Stolen Whinnies

Stolen Whinnies

Wendi Threlkeld

fromtheranchwithlove.com 2021

fromtheranchwithlove.com
fromtheranchwithlove@gmail.com

This is a work of fiction. Names, characters, businesses, places, events, locales, and incidents are either the products of the author's imagination or used in a fictitious manner.

Quote "There's never been a night that could defeat a sunrise or a problem that could defeat hope" in the text is a paraphrase of the quote "There was never a night or a problem that could defeat sunrise or hope" by Bernard J. "Bern" Williams (1913-2004).

Cover by MoorBooks Design.

Cataloguing in Publication Data

Names: Threlkeld, Wendi.
Title: Stolen whinnies / by Wendi Threlkeld
Description: Georgetown, TX : fromtheranchwithlove.com, 2021. |
Summary: A prized miniature horse survives a cougar attack and becomes an unlikely source of hope and healing for a young boy and girl.
Identifiers: LCCN 2021900383
ISBN 978-1-7361772-0-4 (paperback) | ISBN 978-1-7361772-3-5 (ebook) | ISBN 978-1-7361772-2-8 (EPUB) | ISBN 978-1-7361772-1-1 (audible)
Subjects: LCSH: Horses—Juvenile Fiction sh2008105775 | Fear--Juvenile fiction |
CYAC: Family life--Fiction | Hope--Fiction | Horses--Fiction | Human-animal relationships--Fiction
BISAC: JUV002130-- JUVENILE FICTION / Animals / Horses | JUV033280-- JUVENILE FICTION / Christian / Inspiration | JUV039060-- JUVENILE FICTION / Social Themes / Friendship
Classification: LCC PZ7.1.H474T7 | LCC PZ10.3.H474T765 |
DDC [Fic]—dc23

For Katelyn

Once a spunky, driven little girl with a stutter, now a young lady fulfilling her dreams by the handfuls.

1

The Attack

G*o. Go. Go.* A dark presence suddenly broke through the moonlight. Winter's four small hooves pushed forward and against the ground to escape it. Full gallop. Her widespread eyes bulged open like large white marbles.

Where are the others? How did I end up alone?

A pair of laser-like dots approached from behind her haunches. *Those dots are the eyes of a creature, and it's gaining on me.* The pulsing of her heart was a throbbing drum.

I know coyotes are out here. Her nostrils flared and snorted. *This doesn't smell like a coyote. But it smells dangerous.* If the moon hadn't been swallowed up by a thick band of clouds, she could've seen it.

For a miniature horse, I'm fast. I've always beat the other yearlings in races through this pasture. Oh Lord, help me win this time! The prize is not that I can brag, but that I can live. Where's my protector, the stallion? Where's the herd? How could they have vanished?

Breathing mixed with the rapid thumping of her hooves made a terrifying, rhythmic melody that abruptly stopped. A high-pitched whinny escaped her throat.

What is this immense pain? Have I been shot? I heard no gunfire. I've been stabbed! No, it's the creature. It's on me!

Winter's enemy attacked by leaping onto the horse's hindquarters then grabbing and clawing onto her neck and chest.

My back. My neck. My side. It's heavy. Maybe 100 pounds. If I can continue to run, maybe it'll fall off. I must whinny for my life. Then the herd will come to my aid. Why can't I cry out? Why can't I make noise? I feel so woozy.

Bits of moonlight cut through the clouds and shown on the ground like flashlight beams. Eerie blue light began to outline the monster.

What? It can't be. It's a cat as large as a human! A dark, hollow sound rolled out of its throat. A growling purr.

Unable to move, Winter's thoughts began to drift. *Why me? I must've been easier to see in the dark than the others. My striking white coat and sparkling blue eyes that are my pride and glory have betrayed me.*

Random memories flashed in and out of her mind. *All my life, I've dreamt of winning horse shows and pleasing Dr. and Mrs. Browning.*

"Winter is the only miniature horse we own that is a direct descendant from the old Spanish

Conquistadors," they had said many times. Their words seemed to float on air.

I am Winter, a prized and rare breed. A Falabella. How can there be any dreams for me now? I'm alone with my biggest fear. A predator too strong for me to escape.

Looking up to the clouds and stars, she wondered, *Where will my help come from?*

2

The Horse Dentist

"This is c-crazy." The wind whipped strings of Carson's brown hair across her face and mouth as she noticed the full parking lot at the county feed store.

"I told you if you didn't pull it back in a ponytail, it would blow in your face all day," Carson's mom said while unbuckling Carson's little brother and sister from their seats in the van.

Carson spit a large strand of hair out of her mouth only to have it flap right back and thought, *I wasn't even thinking about my hair.*

"M-Mom, look." Because of Carson's stutter it was faster for her to point to the overflow of cars parked on the grass than to describe it.

"Oh wow, this is crazy." Carson's mom echoed.

Carson wondered, *Did all these people get up early on a Saturday to hear a guy talk about miniature horses' teeth? Mom said I would for sure be the only 12-year-old girl interested in the topic, but I never imagined so many grownups would be here.*

She pulled the heavy glass door open and leaned against it, so her mom could corral Franny and Bubba inside. As other folks sauntered inside to hear the monthly guest speaker, Carson sighed, obliged to continue holding the door.

A man about her grandpa's age walked in with another customer and grinned at her. "Thank you, little missy. Are you here to listen to the horse dentist?"

Carson started to answer, then realized that although the "little missy" part was for her, the question part was for the other adult, who replied, "Yep. I imagine he's more a curiosity than anything."

The first man took off his cap and scratched his head. "He may know a thing or two. After all, I've never seen more than 20 people at one of these events."

A curiosity? Carson wondered, feeling a little dismissed by the two men. She was here to learn what the speaker had to say just like they were. *Hey, why am I still here holding the door?* Carson zipped through the store and squeezed through the crowd to the front.

Slowly, all the chatter died down, and the speaker began his presentation.

"Up to 40 teeth crowd and fight for space in a miniature horse's mouth. It's a dental challenge for sure. Add to this equation that a lot of these horses are rescues from folks who throw them out to pasture for years and never check on 'em. Right there's the potential for everything from colic to lameness."

The dentist looked directly into the eyes of everyone standing in the front row and said, "Whoever said 'Never look a gift horse in the mouth' was a fool. When you adopt a pony or a mini, look in his mouth. It's the first thing you better do. Fixin' his teeth could save his life."

"Carson," her mom said in a hushed voice from behind, trying not to distract people from the speaker. Carson glanced over her shoulder.

Franny, her baby sister, was sweaty and red-faced from wiggling about. Her thin, curly hair stuck flat to her damp head as she practiced her goat and chicken sounds with the dedicated passion of a professional opera singer. At her mom's knee was Carson's four-year-old brother. One of his hands grabbed Mom's shirt while the other pinched his nose closed.

Bubba's clearly not a fan of the smells in here, Carson thought. She was accustomed to the familiar feed store smell. Odors from garden fertilizer, animal feed, and chicks in cages, all mixed together.

Carson noticed out of the corner of her eye that Bubba was in his tiny-researcher mode. He brought various kinds of shoveling and scooping tools to his mom's attention. His little eyebrows wrinkled, showing the serious nature of his questions. He insisted on knowing what each tool was for—and couldn't he pleeease have at least one to take home?

"Carson," her mom repeated a little louder than Franny's "baaaaah, baaaaaaah" sheep sounds. "We're going to the back aisle to see the baby chicks and rabbits. You stay and listen." Carson nodded, impressed with her mom's stealthy child-wrangling techniques.

"Quack! Quack! Quack!" Franny said while pinching her nose shut to get the full authentic sound.

Wow, I have to admit, that kid legitimately sounds like a duck. I guess she'll fit right in on that back aisle.

Bubba's voice faded in the distance. "Well, why can't I have a goat pooper scooper? It's a lot smaller than the one for cows. It would take up less room. Mom, I really, really need one of these! I promise I won't ask for anything else for a whole year."

Carson soaked up every word the horse dentist said. When she was in second grade, she'd seen a miniature horse small enough to be carried around like a baby. Her obsession with tiny equines began that day.

The horse dentist's presentation was wrapping up, and a line started to form in front of him. As each person greeted him, they shook his hand then called him either Macky or Mr. McClellan. Carson got a feeling that the folks who called him Macky were friends of his.

Carson had always sensed things about people and relationships. Now that she was older, she was more aware of this ability. For instance, the folks who called the dentist Macky appeared happier and more relaxed around him. The ones who called him Mr. McClellan seemed in a hurry to ask him a question or two and stood straighter while discussing things with him.

Often in a group of people this size, she could easily pick out the ones a little sad or having a bad day from the others.

It's hard to believe how many people are lined up to speak with him. I wonder if all these questions are about miniature horses' teeth. Good grief, how many questions about horse teeth can there be? Carson giggled quietly to herself.

While standing in line to meet the dentist, Carson's thoughts drifted to the horse she was babysitting. *That copper-colored horse is tiny but just as majestic as any fancy show horse I've seen. That is, until she shows off her teeth. So far, anyone who's seen her goofy, big, squared-off grin has practically fallen to the ground laughing. I would never laugh like that at a person, but horses don't care if you laugh at them. It doesn't hurt their feelings at all. It seems like they actually enjoy it.*

A voice caught Carson from behind. "Hi. Do you have a mini or something? Kids never come to listen at these things, except you." Carson spun around and saw a boy about her age.

Shoot. Now I have to talk to him. He's sure to notice my stutter. Okay. Deep breath. Maybe he won't think I'm dumb. You got this, Carson.

"I-I'm w-watching a mini f-for a friend."

"Cool." A big smile crept across his face. His smile was a little higher on the right side of his face than his left, which also made his right eyebrow a bit higher than the other one.

Hmmmm. Carson's people senses kicked into gear. *I like his smile. I feel comfortable around him.*

He had more questions. "Do you get paid to board the mini at your barn?"

"W-we just feed her in our b-backyard." *Take a breath, Carson, and your stutter will stop.* "W-we don't really board her, but I do get paid."

He must have noticed the stutter by now. Carson looked to see if he felt less at ease around her. Nope. The conversation kept rolling along without a hitch.

"That's legit. It's hard for kids our age to make money. My pop and I have been here all morning." He said while pointing his thumb back at the horse dentist. "Did you know they have cookies in the back? You want to go get one?"

Holy cow! The horse dentist is his dad? Lucky kid. Now I'm committed to have a full conversation with this guy.

"Th-That's your dad?" Carson asked, deliberately not answering his question, because she didn't want a cookie. She wanted to know everything there was to know about miniature horses, and his dad was clearly an expert.

Still grinning and quite at ease he said, "Yep. See, these are his business cards. I help him hand them out." He placed one in her hand.

"I have cards too, with Goodness on th-them." She held one directly in front of his eyes. He looked confused until he read the card aloud.

"Goodness, the horse with heart." Jackson looked up. "Goodness is her name? Why does she have her own cards?"

Carson thought, *Usually people stop asking me questions when they hear me struggle to get some of my words out, but not this guy. It's like he's just getting warmed up. And I guess he's one of those smiley kinds of guys, because he keeps smiling away. Even his chestnut-brown eyes seem to be smiling.*

Before she could answer his question about the cards he said, "Hey, let's show the card to my pop."

The line of people was gone. Carson glanced at Goodness on the card to see if her teeth were showing. Of course, they weren't.

What was I thinking? Would a mini horse really flash a big toothy grin full of those huge squared-off chompers like my little sister does every time someone puts a camera in front of her face? The thought made her chuckle a little. That would be a great trick. Everyone would get a good belly laugh out of it.

Suddenly, there they were, planted right in front of the horse dentist. He was sitting on a wooden stool, face to face with them.

"Hey Jackson, who's this young lady with you here?" He leaned forward and rested his elbow on his knee. The smile left Jackson's face for the first time. Carson could tell he wasn't sad or anything. He seemed slightly embarrassed. It was because he hadn't introduced himself or asked her name.

"I-I'm Carson," she blurted out, trying to ease the awkwardness for Jackson. *Normally people try to ease the awkwardness for me when I speak. What a fun twist.*

The horse dentist didn't change his demeanor at all when she stuttered. It was like he didn't notice, exactly like Jackson hadn't. The expert reached out to shake her hand, like he had with all the adults. His hands were scratchy and extra brown, with curly fuzz on top, more like a cowboy's hand than a dentist's.

"Nice to meet'cha, Carson." A big smile crept across his face, precisely like Jackson's. "You have quite a fancy name, young lady, just like the famous Kit Carson."

Carson nodded and offered a controlled smile. She was trying to contain her excitement, or it might be too much for the moment. *This guy's the real deal. He even knows the old-west character Kit Carson. No one ever puts that together with my name.*

Carson handed him the Goodness card.

"What have we here?"

"Pop, she's keeping this mini horse for a friend. She came to hear you talk."

"That's mighty fine. I'm glad you did."

He looked over the three-inch by four-inch trading card and read aloud, "Goodness - a horse with heart." The dentist winked towards Carson and his son. "Looks like we have a celebrity horse here. It says she's a therapy horse."

"Y-yes. And her teeth are f-fine." *Gosh, Carson, she thought to herself. 'And her teeth are fine?' What a dumb thing to say.*

"Well, I bet they are, with you looking after her," he said.

"Peep, peep, peep."

That would be my little sister approaching. Dang. I can't get over how good she is at these animal noises! Carson turned around.

The peeping was coming from a box she was holding. No wonder it sounded so real. It was! The fluffiest, puffiest, fuzziest little peeping chick was inside. She pushed the box right between the horse dentist and Carson, and announced in a loud toddler voice, "Bubba Scooper!"

Carson looked at Bubba. No, he wasn't leaving the store with a scooper. In Franny's little-sister way, she was explaining her victory. Instead of buying a goat pooper scooper for Bubba, the family would be leaving the feed store with a baby chick. Her little brother had acted fairly content until Franny's bold "Bubba Scooper" proclamation.

Grabbing the box out of her hands, he said slowly and with conviction, "This is not a scooper, it's a chick!"

"Bubba scooper, bubba scooper," she said as quickly as she could. Carson recognized that look in her sister's glistening eyes.

Franny's a little thing, but she knows how to get a big reaction out of our normally calm-natured brother.

Carson looked at Jackson and the dentist. They seemed to be relaxed and enjoying the show. Bubba's eyes squinted almost shut as he stared directly at his sister, as if he were trying to melt her face with sheer will power. Franny squealed.

Carson's mom spoke up. "I'm so glad you got a chance to meet Mr. McClellan, Carson. I'm afraid we have to get these guys home, though." She turned to Jackson and his dad. "Thank you so much." Carson read her body language. It was definitely time to go.

"Bye." Carson waved.

"Bye," Jackson replied. "If you ever need Goodness's teeth looked at, give us a call." He displayed one of his dad's business cards in his hands as if it were part of a magic-show presentation. That carefree grin remained on his face the whole time.

What a genuinely friendly guy. Carson loved thinking with big words, like genuinely, but spoke with smaller and simpler words, because she never knew when a word would get caught and stumble on her tongue. Nothing like a stutter to make a great word lose its punch.

I wonder if he lives close by. I bet he'd be fun to hang around. I think he'd be impressed with my friend's mini horse. Maybe he'll get to meet Goodness one day.

While riding home, Carson looked in the back seat at her sister nodding off to sleep and her brother. He was holding the peeping chick with quite a confused look on his face, as if to say, "Now how in the world did this happen?"

In the middle of deep sleepy breaths Franny suddenly mumbled, "Bubba scooper." And just like that, her head dropped. She was sound asleep.

The rest of the family erupted into laughter. Carson had to put her hands on her cheeks because they hurt from laughing so much. *I wonder if Jackson's cheeks hurt from being so smiley all the time.*

"You know," Mom said with a twinkle in her eye, "we're going to have to name that chick Bubba Scooper." Carson nodded and giggled again. Maybe purchasing Bubba Scooper instead of a real pooper scooper wasn't such a bad idea after all.

3

Winter's Angel

With the heavy mountain lion upon her back, Winter sensed the animal's head shift, as it turned its gaze toward the distant barn, where a light popped on. Throngs of pain in Winter's sides and back eased as the creature withdrew its claws.

Finally, the attack has stopped. But why? Does it think I'm as good as dead? Winter locked her knees. *I'm determined to stand, even to the end.*

What's that rustling? Oh no! Another beast is approaching with lightning speed. It can't be old Doc Browning driving his four-wheeler from the barn. The sound is much too quiet and low to the ground. Besides, I haven't seen Doc out here since he started breathing out of that backpack machine a few weeks ago. They call it his oxygen.

The cougar slid off Winter's back and readied itself for battle by letting out a screech of pure terror.

The blood-curdling sound thundered through the horse's bones. The cat's jaws opened. White, wet, fangs were revealed. The skin on its nose stayed rippled with aggression.

Because of the cat's defensive stance, it occurred to Winter that whatever was headed their way must be equally as fierce. A deep growling sound flew toward them from across the pasture.

I actually think that...that's barking. I can't believe this. Can it possibly be Angel?

The stallion says Angel is our watchdog and protector, but he always appeared more like a giant, white, fluffy puppy to me. Ever since I was born last year, he's enjoyed pawing at me and taunting me to run laps with him. I don't know what to think of him now.

Winter remained frozen in the moonlight. Those muscles! I've never noticed Angel's huge, powerful muscles. With unrelenting growls, the dog crouched low, then leaped into battle without hesitation.

Mrs. Browning always called the dog her Sweet Angel Cakes. *What would the dear old Mrs. Browning think of her Sweet Angel Cakes now? I'm glad that monstrous canine is on my side.*

I should run to the barn now that I have the chance—but something about the way the cougar tore my muscles won't let me go forward. If I could only make it to my safe and warm wooden stall.

Winter's breathing became shallow and quick, like the ticking of a wind-up timer. *I don't want to watch this bloody battle between Angel and that beast; yet, here I am. The sole spectator. I'm starting to feel as though I'm almost not even here.* The little horse fell into a trance-like state. *Am I dying?*

Feeling numb, Winter found herself thinking about what was happening to her as an unaffected observer, like someone who narrates a movie. *There's clearly not an ounce of fear in Angel. Wow, he's the one attacking now, at every opportunity. Even between powerful swipes from the lion's large paws.* The giant cat looked back and forth between Winter and the fierce dog. Angel took the moment to go into the fight harder and tried to clamp down on the cat's face.

Out in the distance two more lights appeared. *Maybe the Brownings will come out with the rifle and get rid of this deadly creature that is shredding Angel.*

Pow! A shot echoed through the night sky. The rifle's sound caused the rolling ball of claws, teeth and fur to come to a stop. Angel's intense eyes were fixed on the cougar. The great Pyrenees hunched down, showing ferocious teeth, ready to attack as soon as he could predict which way the mountain lion would go.

The cat-beast made one more evil screech while baring its blood-covered fangs, then melted into the dark abyss behind the trees and pasture fences. Courageous Angel remained in a ready position while guarding Winter. Angel stood his ground as if claiming it while he panned the darkness.

Finally, the head beams of Doc Browning's four-wheeler broke through the heavy night. His deeply treaded tires dug into the earth as they stopped right in front of Winter and her champion, Angel. Once Angel laid eyes on his master, he changed from guardian and protector to loyal servant. Winter watched as he fell limp to the ground and whimpered in pain.

Doc glanced at the scene. "Oh, my Angel, come on boy, what have we here? You've certainly done battle with some creature." Doc looked at Winter's shaking body, and all the bleeding, especially from her neck.

Conjuring up a throaty yell, he pointed his rifle into the sky. "Where are ya?" Gasping for breaths, he sat down and grabbed his oxygen pack. He fumbled around with a clear piece of tubing attached to his backpack and settled it under his nostrils. The oxygen made a kind of hissing, breathing sound as it released the life-giving air. After four long breaths he set the rifle down at his side.

Winter gathered her energy as she neighed at Doc Browning. *I need help. How long is he going to sit there?*

What was that? Was that grunting sound from me? I sound like—like a pig! Try again, Winter.

Doc immediately turned toward the little horse. "Well, listen to that," the old doc said under his breath while slowly standing and walking her way.

Even in Winter's state of trauma she could read Doc's glare and understand his feelings. All the miniature horses could. At this moment, his soft and intense eyes showed compassion from a heavy heart. He firmly placed the palm of his hand in front of Winter's face. This was the "stand" cue.

Winter knew exactly what it meant, and her body complied instantly. Still in somewhat of a trance, Winter remembered when the cue was taught to her.

"Stand, Winter," Doc had instructed, "so when you go to horse shows, you won't fidget. Then the judges will give you high marks for your beauty and excellent proportions."

No one is judging my beauty now.

"Whoa there, little Winter. Whoa, girl. Slow that breathing down, you've lost a lot of blood. We need to make sure it's stopped, but we need to make sure your heart doesn't. Hang on, girl."

What is that he's pulling out of his shirt pocket? I've seen the vet use those on us. They usually push them into our neck muscles, and it feels like a horsefly bite. He's holding the long slender thing in one hand and rubbing my neck with the other. Strange how I don't care. I don't even feel it. I don't feel anything.

###

"Alright, little Winter, this will take the edge off your pain," Doc said as he pulled the needle out, "and hopefully keep you from going into shock. And good Lord, we need to take care of your neck."

Turning his head to the great Pyrenees, Doc shook his head. "And Angel, what a brave warrior you were tonight. Now let me get ya on the back of this ATV."

Carefully, he dragged the fallen soldier onto a lift on the back of the vehicle. "You didn't give up your post. Did ya boy? Be brave just a little longer. You know Mrs. Browning will want her Angel Cakes back home safe and sound."

Doc was hungry for air after dragging the huge dog. He sat on the ATV and took deliberate, deep breaths. Grabbing his phone out of his pocket he muttered, "I've got to get some help out here real fast."

The lit-up screen of his phone was a bright beacon in the dark pasture. He swiped and touched it a few times then began his plea for assistance. "Hello, Dr. Schultz, I'm sorry to bother you at three in the morning, but I'm afraid I need your help, and I need you to do whatever you can to get here right now...

"What? No, I don't have time to text you a picture of this mess. Two of my best animals just got shredded to pieces by some wild dogs, or maybe coyotes. It's Angel and one of our yearlings....

"Yeah, yeah.... It is. Yep, a real shame. Meet me in the pasture to the right of the barn. You'll see the headlights on the four-wheeler....

"No, I'm not going to bring Angel up to your vet clinic. If I leave this little horse out here alone, she'll be a goner for sure. Those animals will come back for her, or she'll die from blood loss. From the look of her, she's in shock. We're going to have to give her meds just to walk her anywhere. Be prepared. It's really bad....

"Thank you. Thank you, Dr. Schultz."

Doc turned to look at Angel and Winter. The retired anesthesiologist was worn out and needed more oxygen to think straight. He looked at Winter and Angel.

"I'm no veterinarian. But I've spent decades in the hospital, working every day with the kind of stuff that could save your lives right now."

His attention turned away from the animals, as he fixed his focus on an area of empty space. In his mind, for a moment, he was back at the supply room of the local hospital.

"It was all right there." Doc motioned in the air as if he were grabbing something he needed off an imaginary shelf. "Dang it all!" he said between coughing fits. "It ain't at my fingertips anymore. Nothin' is."

4

Captain Mom

"Good m-morning Jackson. You're up early," Jackson's mom said loudly from the kitchen, so he could hear her from the living room.

The flight that brought him home to El Paso from Central Texas last night arrived late. It was close to midnight before they pulled into their driveway near the army base at Fort Bliss.

Jackson was proud of himself. As long as he could get himself up in the morning and ready for school without her help, he could name his own bedtime. *Mom's always concerned I'm not getting enough rack time,* Jackson thought. *But the simple truth is, I don't need as much sleep as she thinks I do. I bet I'll get some heat from her within ten minutes because I'm already on the computer, though.*

Still yawning every couple of minutes, Jackson was determined to get up early enough to be ready for school and have time to check out his favorite websites. While flying home last night, he discovered the trading card Carson gave him had a web address at the bottom.

"Let's see, animaltherapywonders.com," he said while pressing the appropriate letters on the keyboard. Jackson thought what his reply would be if challenged about his time on the computer. "Oh yeah, not a problem," Jackson said quietly to himself. "This will for sure count as educational research."

Jackson's mom was an army captain, so he learned quickly which lines not to cross. Once he asked her, "But what if the line isn't clear, and it's more like a long smear mark?"

She gave him a wink and said, "Step on the smear, be grounded for a year." The wink was her way of saying, Not really, but don't push me.

Jackson loved how fast the WiFi around Ft. Bliss was because of all the army technology. A stark contrast to the slow speeds he'd endured driving on the backroads of Texas all week with his pop. Instantly, the screen lit up with pictures of miniature horses of all colors, and people of all ages.

Oh, I can't believe it! Carson's right on the homepage standing next to Goodness. At the bottom of the page, it looks like real-time conversations have been going on. Oh, I see! This is an interactive blog. How cool.

"Mom! Mom!" He shouted down the hallway. "You can see Carson on this website. I mean, on this educational site."

Jackson's mom came down the hallway with the familiar sound of her leather-bottomed army boots scuffing across the wooden floor. She held her favorite stainless-steel travel mug full of hot, black coffee in one hand. It displayed the words Army Strong. Leaning over her son's shoulder she asked, "Which one is Carson?"

"You have to wait a second. It's like a slideshow scrolling through about ten different pictures."

Jackson's mom pointed to the screen. "Is that one him, your b-buddy who has a stutter, like me?" Jackson looked at his mom and felt like she hadn't been paying attention to their conversation on the way home last night.

He sighed. *I clearly talked about Carson like she was a girl. Oh boy, this is going to be awkward now. I don't understand why it has to feel weird to have a really good friend who happens to be a girl.*

"Mom," he said as if the word mom was pronounced longer than it really is. Then he firmly pointed at the computer just as Carson's picture scrolled across. "That's Carson."

His mom stood up straight and took a step back while she held her coffee with both hands. "Carson's a girl. And a really c-cute one, too."

Jackson didn't want to talk about this much, since the school bus was about to arrive. All he had time to do was give her the eye. When she talked about things that made him feel frustrated or awkward, he turned his head toward her, set his jaw to one side, opened his eyes wider than usual, then purposely moved his eyes dramatically toward her direction. It wasn't a mean look. It was just, well, the eye. Sometimes she chuckled and backed off after seeing it.

Just as Mom was noticing the eye, the screech of large tires and the sound of hissing air brakes made them all too aware that the morning school bus had arrived. Immediately, they went into task mode.

"I can't believe you're not out there getting on the bus right now!"

"It's okay Mom, everything's ready here by the door."

Swooping up his backpack, Jackson practically leapt out the door. "I got it. See ya."

"Outstanding, Jackson! Love ya." Mom's words followed him to the bus. Mom and her army buddies labeled anything well-planned as outstanding. And Jackson loved hearing that word.

Leaning his head against the school-bus window, he began to think through the past day's events. It was a great time with Pop during spring break. Traveling with him on his circuit to different locations, bringing comfort and relief to little horses and their owners. And meeting new friends, like Carson. But, it's nice to be back home with Mom too.

Switching between Pop and Mom can feel like one of those amusement park rides that turns a corner so fast your head feels like it's going to jump off your shoulders. Everything about Pop is slow and relaxed, while Mom makes sure our days are filled with tasks that are numbered, sorted and prioritized. Sometimes she even gets out a stopwatch to see how fast we can do things. She can't go to sleep until each task has been completed in order.

Jackson often looked back on what she accomplished in one day's time and thought, *Wow! That's Captain Mom. She's amazing.*

The bus driver grabbed a handle that pulled the vehicle's yellow, folding doors open for another group of kids to come aboard. Jackson smelled a hint of exhaust before the doors closed. The diesel engine revved, nearing the school.

Sorting through more thoughts, Jackson realized a lot of his friends travelled back and forth from their mom's to their dad's homes.

But none of them had a great dad quite like his. *We go all sorts of places together.* He thought about the fancy, huge show barns and rickety old farms, some that had probably been there for a hundred years or more. *And we have good friends in all those places.*

I'll be with Pop in a few weeks for Easter break, and we'll visit some of our friends on his circuit. Maybe we'll see Carson. Jackson almost always visited his father on long weekends like Easter.

Then out of nowhere Jackson thought, *I don't know why Mom and Pop really got divorced. Oh, I know what they told me. But it isn't a real reason.*

They said they like each other better when they aren't married. I think that's about the stupidest reason I've ever heard. I know better than to tell them that, but I wish I was brave enough to say it.

5

The Pecking Order

"Be careful, Carson," Daddy said as Carson headed outside in her pajamas to feed Goodness. "Don't let that horse step on your feet. She may be small, but it would still hurt. One of your pretty little pink toes could pop right off!"

She twirled through the kitchen, grabbed a slice of apple from the breakfast table, then opened the back door. It was time for her to take care of the celebrity horse in her backyard.

"Oh D-Daddy," Carson sighed while pointing her toe at him like a ballerina. This ballerina wore cowgirl boots, her go-to shoes. With her toes safe and sound under the tough leather, Carson didn't worry about stepping on critters or critters stepping on her. And after all, boots look good with anything, from pajamas to her best church dresses.

Closing the patio door behind her, Carson smiled and crouched down as the tiny copper-colored horse pricked her ears toward her. Excited, the mare trotted right over and abruptly froze in place like a statue inches from Carson's face.

There they were, eye to eye. Carson could see her own reflection in one of the horse's dark eyes. Goodness had no idea how goofy and unnatural she looked trying so hard not to move the slightest bit. *Too bad she doesn't know how to play freeze tag,* Carson thought. *That would be hilarious!*

Carson's training was paying off. Goodness could be still for longer and longer periods of time. "Goodness, when you go on that visit to the children's hospital no one will have to worry about their little toes getting stepped on."

Carson couldn't help but laugh at Goodness's intensity. It reminded her of how goofy her little sister looked waiting on everyone else to finish dinner so she could finally have dessert. You could almost see steam burn off the top of her head.

Goodness stood perfectly still while Carson tested her patience. First, she kissed her on the muzzle, then swished her tail around with her hand, and finally circled her three different times doing ballerina twirls. "Oh, look at those ears," Carson said. "Someone is finally getting a tad impatient."

The horse's ears went from a pricked up straight stance to a laid back, almost flat position. When horses are really mad, their ears press down completely flat against the back of their heads. Carson had always been good at reading people's behavior. She welcomed the challenge of learning animal behavior too.

"Goodness," Carson said, needing to keep the horse focused, "listen to me. Stay still." Carson used to wonder why she never stuttered when instructing Goodness. Perfect S and T sounds easily flow forward. But now, she just rolls with it.

She circled the horse one more time, then gave her the delicious prize for her obedience, the golden apple slice. Carson remembered what Goodness's owner had taught her: "The key in training patience is to push her longer than she wants to be pushed, but not so long that it exasperates her."

Alright, time to scoop the poop, Carson thought. Wherever horses are, muck isn't far behind their behinds. *Where is that mucking shovel? My tool-obsessed little brother must have played with it yesterday after Mom wouldn't buy him his own scooper.* A grin crept onto Carson's face as she remembered how it went down.

Did we really bring home a little yellow chick and name him Bubba Scooper? Carson chuckled.

Walking back into the kitchen, Carson found Daddy trying to convince Mom to buy more chicks, while two-year-old Franny meowed over and over like a kitten crawling on the floor. *And is that really a saucer of milk someone placed on the floor for her to lap up? Good grief, one of the adults in this house is getting soft.*

Carson's brother had found everything in the house that in any way resembled a scooper, including soup spoons, ladles, and measuring cups. He carefully lined them up from largest to smallest, with a glaring empty spot where the goat pooper-scooper would have fit in perfectly, if it had been purchased instead of the chick.

Interestingly enough, the only out–of-the-ordinary thing about all this activity was that Daddy actually wanted more chicks. This was so shocking because Carson knew he probably didn't want Bubba Scooper to begin with.

Daddy always says any animal brought home is a responsibility not to be taken lightly. Carson had heard him more than once say he already has plenty of responsibility keeping up with all of them. *Why is he trying to convince Mom to go get chicks? I've got to find out.*

"I know this seems crazy, but you'll just have to go get a couple more of those chicks or take this one back," Daddy said while refilling Franny's milk saucer on the floor.

"Okay. Don't worry. I'll take care of it today," Mom said. "I had no idea chickens were so awful to each other."

"M-mom, what do you m-mean?"

"I bought Bubba Scooper thinking we could use him to draw your brother's attention into some of our life-science classes."

Carson felt lucky that her mom was a science professor. When Mom found out how much Carson loved science, the two of them were unstoppable. At the age of twelve, Carson had already completed every middle-school level science class and was almost finished with high-school biology.

Mom continued, "Once we'd finished the unit on birds, I was going to take our little object lesson, Bubba Scooper, to the neighbor's chicken coop to live."

Carson knew who Mom was talking about. One of the driveways near their house had a sign next to a mailbox that said Farm Fresh Eggs. Lots of chickens equal lots of eggs. Carson had seen her mom pulling up social media posts of these chickens on her phone. Her mom had searched for a chicken dinner recipe by typing in #warmingupchicken. What popped up was the neighbor holding her chickens in hand knit sweaters. Mom said the neighbor was eccentric and interesting.

Carson's mom continued, "Daddy just explained to me that once you have a group of chickens you can't introduce a new one very easily. The others usually attack it."

Carson spun on her heels to face Daddy. "What? That sounds like an awful reality show, Chickens in Sweaters B-Behaving B-Badly."

"It's true, Carson. Have you ever heard of the phrase, pecking order?"

She nodded.

"This is the exact scenario that phrase comes from. Chickens aren't like people. You can't just dress them in sweaters, tell them to examine their conscience, and expect them to stop being mean to each other. They will always have a pecking order. The chicken that is strongest and in charge is at the top and the weakest, or youngest, or newest is at the bottom. If a chick comes into a coop with no mother to protect it, it will most likely get pecked to death."

Suddenly Daddy had a captive audience. The entire family was staring at him with their mouths hanging wide open in disbelief. Well, at least it was disbelief from Carson. Franny soon turned back around and picked up meowing where she had left off.

Bubba took in the harsh news, and then went back to organizing his scoops and measuring cups.

Heartbroken, Carson asked, "Won't one of the hens adopt the baby? Won't the rooster protect him?" She felt a strange mixture of sadness and anger well up inside.

"No, honey, not usually. I've never seen it happen. There's no way to protect the chick. But if a group of them grow up together, they establish their own pecking order without killing each other."

How could this be? Carson had flashbacks to all the feature films she had seen about farms and all the children's books she'd checked out from the libraries over the years. Those fuzzy, sweet, little peepers, the gallantly handsome roosters, and the kind mother hens. Not one single story had ever taught the pecking order concept. She felt she'd been lied to by every author who ever wrote a song, book, or cartoon about chickens on a farm.

Furthermore, how could the Texas Farm & Feed Store let them leave the premises with a peeping box without giving a proper warning? *How irresponsible of them,* Carson thought. *Maybe there's some kind of required government warning on the box we brought Bubba Scooper home in. Maybe I just missed it.*

"Mom, where is the b-box that Bubba Scooper came home in?"

"Carson, he's still in it. It's right over there."

Indeed, there was a label on the lower left-hand corner of the box! *Maybe they're responsible citizens after all, and I just neglected to read the warning.* Carson could hear the sweet little chirpy peeps as she picked up the box to read the words.

Let's see. Clear as day, the label states:

Thank you, I've found a home!
This box is made from recycled materials

"Mom!" Carson announced with a sense of urgency as she marched toward the front door to get in the car. "I am c-coming with you. Bubba Scooper's life d-depends on it!"

"Okay, superhero of all that is right and true in the animal kingdom; but first, I think you should trade your ruffled nightgown for some blue jeans and a shirt if you want them to take you seriously at the feed store."

In the car, as the motor quietly hummed, Carson thought about Jackson and his dad, the horse dentist. "M-Mom, I w-wonder if the horse dentist and Jackson will be doing another clinic today."

"I don't think so, Carson. At least I know Jackson won't be. I heard the man at the checkout counter say the dentist's son was here with his dad because he was on spring break from El Paso. Today's Monday; I'm sure he had to be back at school."

"How f-far is El Paso? Is it very far?"

"Good heavens, yes. You have no idea how big Texas is until you have driven from just about anywhere in the state to El Paso."

Carson's mom watched as Carson sighed and sank into the seat. "You two kind of hit it off, didn't you? The man in the back of the feed store sure had a lot of really kind things to say about Jackson's dad. In fact, it sounds like his dad is kind of a famous character in the mini-horse world."

"M-mom, you know what Daddy said about the p-pecking order?" Mom nodded, keeping her attention on the road. "Daddy said chickens aren't like p-people. They have to b-be mean to each other." Mom nodded again as she pulled into a parking space at the Texas Farm & Feed Store. "B-but, sometimes p-people are like chickens. They can be mean to each other and p-push the newest or youngest ones around."

"You're right about that, sweetie. It is very unfortunate. Have you seen people treat each other like that?"

Carson nodded.

"You know Carson, one of my favorite quotes is by President Roosevelt's wife. Her name was Eleanor. She said, 'No one can make you feel inferior without your consent.'"

Sitting quietly for a minute, Carson let those words sink into her head, because Mom had that smug teacher look on her face, like after she introduced a fundamental math concept. Then Carson finally blurted out, "Well w-what in the world is that supposed to mean?"

Carson's mom smiled. "It means sometimes humans will try to push you around by saying things that hurt you and make you feel ugly, unimportant, or dumb. But who are they to say anyone is smarter or more important than you? Walk tall and confidently because the truth is, everyone is created and loved by God equally.

"So, the hurt they intend to cause will do nothing. Because you hold the power to let it affect you or not by the way you receive those words. We also need to remember that it doesn't matter if people are rich or poor, or what they look like...or if they excel in math or science." She winked at Carson as she said that last part.

"What Mom? What was that wink for?"

"Sweetheart, you know you are a natural at math and science. Far beyond your grade. But if you tell people about that a lot, it can make people who struggle in those subjects or even people who are doing fine at grade level, feel not very smart. Because they compare themselves to you."

"Am I supposed to k-keep it a secret? Why do I have to k-keep something a secret that I love?"

"Carson, I didn't say anything about keeping secrets. Of course, you should talk about matters that interest you. Just stay humble, my girl."

Carson thought about Eleanor's quote. *No one can make you feel inferior without your consent.*

"Mom, when I met Jackson, he made me feel the opposite of inferior. I felt smart and important. I think he was the nicest new f-friend I've ever made."

6

Tough Decisions

"Schultzie, I can't believe we got this little horse to walk as far as the barn," Doc Browning said with hungry breaths of air. "That shot calmed her nerves right down." He pointed to a miniature-sized horse trailer beside the barn. "You can load her up in that trailer. I'll have to meet you at the vet hospital after I rest a little while and catch my breath."

The young country vet took a long breath himself and gathered his thoughts for a minute. "Look, Doc Browning, I don't know how to say this, but you really already said it yourself. I don't think this little horse can make it any further either."

"Now wait just a minute, Schultzie. You gave her the meds to get her this far. You can see as plain as I can. Her jugular and carotid arteries are still intact. If the damage had been one hair closer to them, she'd already be gone. The bleeding is under control. I know

I'm no veterinarian but give me some credit here. In my medical opinion she could pull through this."

"Doc, look at the tissue damage." The two men gazed at the skin and muscles that had been torn off Winter's back and neck.

"If she doesn't have a heart attack right now, she'll likely die of infection. If she survives that, she will suffer the rest of her life from muscle damage. She'll for sure be lame. Let her go, Doc. She's suffering here. Let me take your dog back with me to the vet hospital. Angel has a real chance."

Doc Browning was skilled at making quick medical decisions for human patients, but for some reason this one about his miniature horse had him stuck, real stuck.

The young vet spoke up. "Doc, Angel has organs exposed here. I have to take him in if he's going to make it. I know this sounds unlikely, but the attack had to be from a mountain lion."

The vet pointed to the claw marks on Winter's hind quarters and the large wound that began at the horse's crest. "Look at your little horse. See the attack patterns here and here. Big predatory cats attack by biting just above the shoulders. And look at these puncture marks where the fangs were, and at her throat."

The slashes around her throat were hard to look at. Doc Browning realized those were why she couldn't make any horse noises. Her voice box was damaged.

"I know you've got bobcats around here too, but no bobcat can produce this much carnage at once. I'll need to let the authorities know as well. This cat could strike again."

Winter looked up at the two men. She had stopped trembling but continued her quick breathing pattern. She was utterly beaten down.

The vet looked the old doctor straight in the eye. "Look at her, Doc. She's exhausted."

"Okay. Alright. Dang it all," he said, not making eye contact with Dr. Schultz. Instead, he was giving Winter a real good look over, really studying her.

"Now Doc, you know I don't normally do this, but because you're an anesthesiologist, I'm going to leave you with the shot to put her down. Put it in her neck and she will go the quickest, but I'm sure you know that."

Doc Browning took the shot from Dr. Schultz and nodded his head, still staring at Winter's injuries.

"Okay, I'm off with Mr. Angel here. Call me if you need anything." The vet had already turned and loaded the heavy dog on a mechanical lift that pulls large animals right into the back of his truck. As he pulled away, he hollered, "I'll let you know how Angel's doing as soon as we get him in stable condition."

###

With a surge of anxiety, Winter's eyes quickly popped wide open. *Something is cold and dripping on me. My hooves, can they move? Can they gallop if I need them to?*

"Alrighty there, little filly, whoa there. This is just Betadine. It keeps the infection risk down. I always carry some in my bag when I'm out here. It's cold and wet. I know it feels scary to you, but it won't hurt a bit."

Winter watched the old doc as he walked out the barn door just to return a few seconds later with a black leather bag. He kept repeating, "Alright little filly," and "Hang on there, little filly."

Winter's thoughts began to scatter. *He hasn't called me that since before Mrs. Browning decided on my name, Winter. That must've been about nine or ten months ago. I think she wanted to be sure my coat would remain white all year before giving me the name.*

White, everything around me seems to be fading to white. I remember that I reminded her of snow. I think I must be drifting to sleep.

Winter thought something in the ol' doc's eyes had changed. He was much different from minutes before. Did he give me that shot the vet left behind?

And just like that, Doc started talking up a storm. Winter didn't know if he was speaking only to her. He seemed to be rambling to the barn cats, to the ceiling, and to someone named Good-Lord-Almighty. He walked around the barn with purpose, keeping the oxygen hooked right up to his nose in order to breathe.

"I may be an old, retired son-of-a-gun, but I think I can save ya," he said, looking in the corners of the barn at some odd things he'd stored away. "I'm gonna need some help, but I won't get it from that vet Schultzie. He's working on my Angel right now anyway. And I know he'll fix our hero up just fine.

"I'm old, and I've got lung cancer. Between you and me, little filly, I struggle every day to forgive myself for the smoking. I, of all people, knew better. And now, I'll be leaving my darling wife of 40 years alone. Every day I chose to smoke, I was choosing to leave her too early in this life.

"Well, one thing's for sure, she's not going to lose you too, Winter. You're going to hang on for us both. You got that?

"If I have the skill and knowledge to save you but not the mercy to actually do it, well then, I might as well already be dead."

Finally, he stopped his confessional to concentrate on breathing. Then he picked up his phone to "call in some favors." Before everything went solid white, Winter wondered who or what those favors would be.

7

Stashing Memories

Carson heard her mom quietly shut her baby sister's bedroom door.

Hooray! Franny's asleep! Finally. naptime is here. Now I can do Carson things without being constantly climbed on and followed.

Carson cherished the time when her thoughts could be her own. For seven years she had been an only child. She truly loved being a big sister, but her time alone was energizing.

Mom peeked around the corner and saw Carson on the computer. "You can recharge your batteries now, Carson. Not only is Franny down but your brother is playing next door."

Until this year, Carson never understood that phrase. Mom would look at her if she acted extra tired or frustrated and say, "It looks like your batteries need recharging." Carson would immediately run to her room and look at all the batteries she could find. They always seemed to be working fine.

Her mom meant she would feel more like herself again if she took some time to be on her own. Carson wondered how many other things her mom and dad said that she misunderstood. *Good grief,* she thought, *why can't people just speak plainly?* Although now that she was figuring some of these sayings out, the double meaning of things was kind of fun.

"M-mom can you believe this? Jackson has some posts on the mini-horse w-website."

"Really? Let me see. He sure does. Wow, he says his mom is a captain in the army. So that explains why he lives all the way out in El Paso."

Carson looked at her mother with questioning eyes. *How did she put those two things together? I wonder what else she'll tell me about Jackson that it doesn't say on the website.*

Carson tried to imagine Jackson sitting down at his computer, putting in all his comments. She was sure he smiled away with every keystroke.

Carson's mom began to read over Carson's shoulder, "Oh look. Jackson's saying, 'My mom works at Fort Bliss.'" She paused and turned toward Carson, "That's the army base in El Paso. Move over a little Carson, so I can read the rest of the screen." Carson scooted over a bit so they could share the office chair.

"He says he hopes his dad can work on Goodness's teeth someday. Look at these pics of him and his dad working on miniature horses' teeth from all over the country.

"Golly, Carson, do you really think Goodness needs dental work? I mean, her teeth are pretty straight. Why do all these horse owners obsess over their horses' teeth? Isn't that kind of strange?"

"M-Mom, horses have to have their t-teeth floated regularly."

"Really? What do they float them on? Water? How does that even work?"

Carson giggled. "M-Mom, it is like h-having their sharp edges shaved off, so their teeth don't scratch and cut the insides of their own m-mouths."

"Wow, I never knew that. Floated. How interesting."

Well, that's a first, Carson thought. *I used a word mom wasn't familiar with, and it had to do with animal science.*

Carson pointed to the screen, showing her mom a cool idea Jackson mentioned on the interactive blog. While reading the screen Mom said, "Oh cool. He liked that trading card you gave him so much he has an idea for another one. One that says—"

Carson interrupted her mom. She wanted to hear herself say it out loud first. "W-we support our troops!"

Carson's mom smiled. "What a great idea! Carson, you've helped with these trading cards before. Do you think you could help with this idea? You know these will be a hit when the therapy horses visit the veterans' hospital."

"Oh Mom, you know I can. I'll sketch out the design right now. It has to have a flag, and Goodness can wear camouflage."

"Why you stutter so little when you're talking about that horse, I'll never know," Mom said as she walked out of the room. "Really Carson, camouflage is even hard for me to say."

Carson had to grin. It was true. She didn't stutter as much when she was caught up in the world of horses. Especially when she trained them.

Brilliant thought coming in, Carson thought. *What if I post a sketch of my trading card ideas on the website?* Carson quickly sketched her idea with a drawing attachment she kept next to her computer. *Alright, now I just need to click, and send. There. It's done.*

Carson thought of how Miss Amy, Goodness's owner, called collecting the trading cards "memory keeping." When people collect the cards, they go back and look at them often. Kind of like when old-timers look at baseball cards from long ago.

The cards trigger fond memories of being part of something special. Miss Amy told Carson it did more than cheer people up. Seeing the horses produced chemicals in their bodies that make what's happening in their brains work better. Work more effectively. Carson loved the science behind the horse therapy.

Everything I've learned to do with Goodness, I remember perfectly, Carson thought. *Maybe I should start doing my math homework with her.* Suddenly, the computer screen made a noise.

Ding. A new entry posted on the website. *Ahhh. What's this? It's Jackson again.* Carson read that he and his dad would be back in the Central Texas area for Easter weekend. Jackson thought all the mini-horse owners in the area might want to know in case their horses needed their teeth floated or any other dental care.

Carson pulled up the calendar on the computer to look at that weekend and noticed Friday was highlighted as a holiday, too. "Mom!" Carson yelled down the hall. "Do kids usually get G-Good Friday off from school? You know, the Friday right before Easter."

"Yes, Carson. They usually do."

Wow, Carson thought. *If he comes in on the night before Good Friday, he could be here in just 16 days!* Carson highlighted the Thursday before Easter on the calendar in pink.

I hope there is some way we can get together. He would go nuts over Goodness in her camo gear. He could have his picture made with her as a surprise for his mom.

A burst of excitement surged through Carson's brain. *That's it! This could be amazing.* Carson loved organizing surprises but rarely had the opportunity. *Oh, we just have to do this! Okay, Carson, calm down and think this through*, she said to herself. *I need to put this on the website without his mom knowing we're putting together a photo shoot. I would hate for her to read it and ruin the moment. She has to know as little as possible. This has the potential to beat my last surprise.*

Carson's last surprise was when she and her mom surprised her brother and sister with Goodness in their backyard. Franny and Bubba wanted to eat dinner and sleep outside. Goodness was the tiniest horse they'd ever seen. Of course, they weren't allowed to sleep outside. So, they cried so hard, that Carson's mom and dad almost had meltdowns themselves. *Wow,* Carson thought, *that was a really great surprise.*

Carson's dad's near meltdown turned to pure joy when he learned they were temporarily keeping the horse and hadn't actually purchased it.

Carson reeled her thoughts back to the most current surprise plan. It involved a Support our Troops therapy-horse trading card, complete with a horse in a camo uniform and army boots. The kicker at the end would be surprising Jackson's mom, the army captain.

This is going to take some clever maneuvering. I hope Jackson's up for it. I can't believe all the fun that happens around miniature horses!

Carson needed to get in touch with Jackson for this to work. *Ah ha!* The horse dentist's business card had a phone number on it. Running to her room, she nearly wiped out on the slick wooden floors because of her cotton socks. Her gaze quickly found the little stack of important things kept wedged in the corner of her dresser. From the pile she pulled Jackson's dad's business card - the horse dentist.

He's not with his dad right now, Carson remembered. She'd read on his post that he was in El Paso with his mom right now. How could this all come together without bringing Jackson in on the planning?

Carson rubbed her thumb over the thick business card with raised letters printed on it.

Alright, Carson thought, *time to put Jackson's dad's business card back into my squirrel stash.*

Carson's mom named it that. The mish mash of tiny toys, broken jewelry, foreign coins, and now a horse dentist's business card found a home together. One of Goodness's trading cards was in the squirrel stash, too. If everything worked out, and it had to, Carson would soon add the best trading card yet.

8

Calling in Favors

"Goliad County Emergency Medical Service, how can I direct your call?"

"This is Dr. William Browning. Is David Bumble on duty tonight?"

"Yes, Doctor."

"Great, put him on."

"One moment please."

A man's voice answered, "This is David."

"Hi, David, this is Dr. Browning. How busy is it down there in the E.R. this morning?"

"Hi, Dr. Browning. It's slow. There's nothing going on at all. How are you these days? What's up?"

"Who's down there with you? Who's on your team this morning?"

"Uh, well there's six of us, sir. I don't think you know any of the others."

"Try me. Who are they? Any locals?"

"Stephanie and Charlie are here. They went to Goliad High School."

"Stephanie Garza?"

"Yes, sir."

"She's the one."

"Pardon me, sir?"

"Ok, listen up. I need you two to take the ambulance on a routine drive. Fill it up with gas. Get its oil changed, pick up sandwiches for the team, whatever. But come by my place first."

"Doc, are you okay? It's no big deal to make this an official run."

"David, listen to me carefully. I'm not in danger, but I need you and Stephanie to run by my barn. I'd rather no one knew about it, but if you're asked, you can say you decided to drop by and check on me before you got the sandwiches, the gas or whatever. Folks will understand, after all we've been through together."

"Yes, Doc. I'll never forget how you kept my son out of pain after that brutal football injury. We didn't think he would ever be able to walk unassisted—"

"Now, David, no need to go bringing all that up. It was an honor to do it. I hate to sound forceful, but I do need this favor quickly. Stephanie will go right along with ya. She's never stopped thanking me after I helped with the triplets' births. We'd never had a set of triplets in our hospital, and I don't think we've had any since."

"No sir. We haven't. I didn't know you were her anesthesiologist for that."

"Well, I don't know how you don't. She announces it to the world every time she sees me or

Mrs. Browning at the grocery store, and those boys must be in high school by now.

"Anyway, make sure you have strong sedatives on board that won't inhibit breathing. I'll also need an I.V. solution for up to 250 pounds, and..."

"Sir?"

"David Bumble, are you writing this down? Stop interrupting me. Okay, where were we? Tons of suturing equipment and a liquid antiseptic, like Betadine. I'll see you in no more than ten minutes. Now get over here, son."

Doc Browning ended the call, and the glow of his cell phone faded. He took several deep breaths and turned toward the miniature horse.

"Little filly, we'll see if this works. I may be an old son-of-a-gun, but I've still got some value in this world. Ninety percent of this town was either born under my watch in the hospital or had their tonsils removed while I kept them unconscious. More importantly, I safely woke them from slumber after their surgeries were over. Truth be told, that's the trickiest part.

"I've seen more accident victims in the E.R. than a man should, and I've seen some amazing medical recoveries that had my name associated with them. You, my dear, are going to be my last one."

As the old doctor scanned Winter's torn up body, he continued to think aloud to her in comforting tones. "I've been looking at your muscle structure, and I think I can make out where everything is supposed to go. I haven't thought about stitches and emergency surgery in decades. Certainly, I've never thought of equine surgery. Good Lord, this is going to be a process indeed."

The horse was covered in sticky blood, sweat and dirt. Her quick shallow breaths seemed to align themselves perfectly with the doctor's old wristwatch as its second hand rhythmically beat out each tiny slice of time. Exactly ten minutes had passed.

The head beams of the emergency vehicle approached and the tires made a crunching, crackling sound on the gravel road as it came to a stop. "Alrighty, they did it," he muttered to himself.

"Winter, you see these two crazy folks coming down the path from that ambulance? David and Stephanie are going to be real helps to us now. Don't you worry. In a couple hours you'll be in full recovery. Mark my words."

9

Jackson

"Jacks, stop staring at the computer screen. It isn't good for your eyes. How long have you been slumped over letting the computer glow off your forehead like that, son?"

"I dunno."

"I've heard screen glow on your forehead has been proven to cause zits to colonize." Jackson's mom flashed half a smile Jackson's direction to let him know she was joking. She continued her morning routine around the house while occasionally texting her army buddies.

Jackson let the screen light mesmerize him. His toes pressed against the floor and rhythmically swiveled his body from left to right in the desk chair. The dim little office without windows suited Jackson's mood.

The therapy horse community website Carson had told him about was up. At least twenty mini horses were registered for a variety of dental procedures—all to be done by his dad in one day. The therapy barn would serve as a temporary dentist's office. The surrounding pasture would offer plenty of space for horse trailers, a sort of waiting room for the equine patients.

Jackson liked how the posting about his dad looked like a movie poster for an old western. It read: "Macky McClellan, the horse dentist - to appear at The Horse Therapy Training Center of Central Texas. Discounted dental treatments given to therapy horses on Good Friday."

Underneath, someone commented, "Will Macky's famous son Jackson be there too?" with a smiley face emoji. Jackson almost smiled. They were Carson's remarks.

He scrolled through the list of horse names and started to read them aloud. "Pixie, Bilbo, Thumbelina, Bucky, Goodness...Goodness is on the list. Yep. Carson will be there."

Jackson wanted to be excited about seeing his new friend, but he wasn't. In fact, since receiving the bad news, he didn't even feel up to lifting his fingers to type a response to her.

Jackson's mom glanced over her shoulder from the hallway and asked, "Are you ready to fly out to Austin tonight? All packed?"

"Yeah."

"Outstanding," Mom said in her Captain Mom voice.

With that, Jackson gave his mom the look and plopped his head down on the desk.

"I know we got some rotten news, son. But Jacks, why don't you at least let Carson know you'll be going to see Goodness with your pop tomorrow? Friends let each other know when they're going to be in town."

Jackson looked over at his mom. His eyes suddenly felt like saturated sponges ready to leak all over the place, and that made him mad. He never seemed to be able to stop the tears when they came. He didn't think guys his age cried anymore. At least the anger pushed the tears back a little.

Jackson had been sad and angry at the same time before, but not like this. The size of this feeling seemed far too big for anyone's heart to hold. How could he explain this to his mom? How can you explain a feeling you can't understand?

Jackson's eye caught one of his favorite photos of himself on the desk. In the clear plastic frame, he stood next to one of his dad's patients, a famous miniature horse from Hollywood.

The horse stayed at his dad's for a couple of weeks for some serious work on a tooth infection. Jackson spent time soothing the horse by brushing and walking him. He remembered thinking the horse could understand his thoughts and feelings–sometimes more than he could understand them himself. It felt good to be truly known, and it felt good knowing the horse wasn't going to blab everything he knew to anyone else. They held secrets together. Secrets that brought healing through a common understanding.

Well, he thought in a burst of internal anger, *Mom doesn't have animals, much less horses. And now I know why. It's hard to care for animals when you aren't even going to be around for a whole year or more.*

Jackson's mom knelt down beside him and quietly said, "Hey Jacks, we are s-strong enough to get through this." She placed her arm on his shoulder. "W-will you give your mom a hug?"

Jackson knew his mom well. Stress was causing that stutter to slip out. He broke his vigilant stare at the photograph and embraced his mom. Being deployed was going to be hard on her, too.

The army captain put down her phone with its occasional chirps from incoming texts. To Jackson, it represented her constant connection to work and friends.

"Jacks, you know the army is important to me. And it's bigger than that."

"I know, Mom. It's our country."

"That's true, son. But also, it's kind of a big deal that the army would let me in and continue to move up the ranks."

Jackson felt unsettled about that. His mom did some crazy hard stuff for the army, including handling all types of foreign money transactions. Her friends called her the army's money ninja. Once, Jackson met a general who singled his mom out to mention how brilliant she was.

"Why, Mom? Did you get in trouble or something?"

Jackson's mom leaned back and raised her eyebrows. "Why, no, Jacks. It's b-because of my stutter. That's considered a disability. I had to work harder and prove myself more to my officers than others did.

I had to show them how much they needed someone like me. I'm pretty good with numbers, ya know."

Jackson thought, *That's an understatement. More like a mastermind.*

"Mom, you can't be serious. Because of your stutter? But how is that even fair?"

"Things are different today than they used to be when the U.S. first organized an army. An army captain back in the day would be out on the field, yelling orders at troops in the middle of bloody battles. And some captains still need to do that today. But we also need a strong leadership presence on the internet and in financial centers around the world."

"Mom, I know you kick butt and take names at that stuff." Jackson's sudden surge of pride in his mom and what she did for the U.S. instantly dried up his emotional, moist eyes.

"I do, Jackson. I do. Wherever the U.S. Army goes, lots of money is involved, and I organize the army's money better than anyone else I know. Right now, some big financial operations are going down, and they need me closer to the action."

"Because you're their money ninja."

"Yes, Jackson. But, I'm your mom too. And we are strong. We've got this."

10

Cell Phones

"Daddy, can I use your cell phone?"

Carson's dad didn't take his eyes off the road or give her an answer, but he didn't stop her from grabbing his phone either. Carson took that as a yes.

"Carson, please stop kicking. What did this poor truck ever do to you?"

Carson glanced down at her feet. She'd been kicking the bottom of the dashboard with the toes of her boots, unaware. Her excitement about the day was coming out her toes.

"We're almost to the horse barn. What time do I need to pick you up?"

Carson made swipe and touch motions on the screen. "Really, Daddy, you should set your apps to automatically update." She sat the phone in her lap for a minute. "Hmm. I don't know. I'm doing more than helping with the horses today. We're t-taking pictures for the new trading card. It's so cool. It's called Support our T-troops."

"Does this have anything to do with why you've been asking everyone if you could borrow some army boots?"

Carson nodded and looked down at the phone again. She hadn't heard from Jackson in the last week or so. *He's got to be here today.* Carson's foot kicked under the dashboard.

Her dad threw a hard look her way and shook his head. The anticipation was making her anxious. *I'm going to text Jackson's pop. I gotta know!*

Carson's dad noticed her carefully typing in a phone number from a business card onto his phone.

"Wait a minute there, li'l missy, who are you texting?" She suddenly felt like her dad didn't trust her, which made her a little confused. Her dad was treating her like he would treat her little sister Franny, who was practically a baby.

"Father, I'm sending a text to Macky McClellan, the—"

Her dad quickly interrupted, "Macky who? Is that who's on that business card? Since when did you start carrying around business cards? And did you just call me Father?"

Carson sat up straight and poised herself for grown-up conversation. She was determined NOT to stutter. *Ok, take a deep breath Carson,* she said to herself.

"Father, I'm practically a teenager and teenagers don't always call their dads, Daddy. It's no b-big deal."

Dang. A little stutter squeaked out.

Carson pointed to the card and concentrated on speaking a little slower to get all the words out clearly. "And Father, this is the horse dentist."

"Well, Offspring," her dad said in a tone that exactly mimicked his daughter's, "I don't think you should be texting businessmen we don't know. In fact, I don't think you need to be texting much at all. Put my phone back, please."

Carson held back a dramatic reaction. That would be something a little girl would do. Instead, she breathed in and out methodically while her insides felt tight and tense. Calmly and coolly, she placed the phone back in her dad's cup holder on his side of the truck.

He doesn't know that Mr. McClellan isn't some strange businessman. And he doesn't even want to hear me explain that either.

Looking out her window and feeling utterly helpless secured a very powerful thought in her head. This was the moment in time when Carson knew beyond a shadow of doubt what she truly needed—and must have as soon as possible: her very own cell phone. No matter how many animal sitting jobs it took, she would make it happen.

Meanwhile, Father, formally known as Daddy just five minutes ago, also had an equally powerful thought. *It's going to be a long time before that li'l missy gets her own cell phone!* And his thought might as well have been poured in concrete and set out to dry in the hot Texas sun.

"Alright, here we are. The Therapy Horse Barn," Carson's dad said. "Give me a kiss, Offspring, and off you go." Carson gave a little smile, leaned over to kiss her dad's sandpaper-like chin, then burst out the door as if she were spring loaded.

11

The Therapy Barn

The sunshine and cool breeze made Carson feel alive. *Look at all those miniature horses!* Some pranced around like noble steeds. Others settled down in corners, searching for delicious spring grass to nibble.

These little guys have no idea how small they are. They just know they're magnificent horses. That lucky Jackson gets to be around these tiny beasts all the time.

Amy Jo, the barn owner, spotted Carson while barking out friendly greetings and instructions to visitors. "Go ahead and park that trailer right there," she hollered. "Yes, go on. Macky's ready for ya!"

"Amy Jo!" Carson said with a beaming smile. "I'm here to help."

"Hi, Carson. Welcome to the circus." They shared a laugh. "Go have fun. Let me know if anyone needs anything. Later, we'll do the soon-to-be famous Support-our-Troops photo shoot."

"Yes ma'am."

Okay. Now to find Jackson. Are there cookies somewhere? That's where he'll be. Carson saw a man bent over a speckled horse's head, working hard at filing down the animal's teeth. *There's Macky.*

Carson wanted to run over and say hello, but she also didn't want to slow him down. She walked to the barn office and saw the photo-shoot station inside, ready to go. She could see a camouflage costume for Goodness and an American flag. *Oh, this is going to be the best trading card ever!*

She remembered the guy at the hardware store saying he wanted twelve to send to all the men who served with him in his unit. At least two of his buddies attended equine therapy for veterans.

They're gonna go nuts over this.

On Amy Jo's desk near the photo station sat a computer. It was open to the therapy horse barn's website. Carson noticed that Amy Jo had approved several new posts a few minutes ago. *Oh snap! Here's one from Jackson.*

Carson paused and swallowed hard. Only two words. She read them aloud.

"BAD NEWS - sad face emoji."

What does that mean?

Mom would be able to figure this out. I need to read between the lines, like she does. Oh my gosh. I think I know! It means Jackson couldn't come this weekend! That has to be the bad news. I thought he said he spends every long weekend with his dad.

Mom said most kids have Friday off before Easter weekend. I bet he didn't get it off. Oh, this is terrible.

Carson felt her face getting hot and flushed. Her plans were going to have to change. That was all there was to it. Time for plan B.

She began to sweat. *But I don't have a plan in place in case my first plan doesn't work. I have one very detailed and perfect plan. Plan A. And plan A has to happen!*

Carson peered around the corner to see how Macky was coming along with the next little horse when a boy with chestnut-colored eyes handed him a water bottle.

Carson, she scolded herself. *You may be really good at reading people's actions and even horse's behavior, but you are definitely not good at reading between the lines.*

She hurried toward Jackson. Finally, time to let him in on the surprise.

Carson had only met Jackson once in person, but she sensed he wasn't himself. He wasn't very smiley, and his whole body seemed a little...slumpy. *Hmm,* she wondered. *What's the bad news?*

As Carson approached the McClellans they seemed very busy and serious with the horses, so she stifled the urge to run and give them big friendly hugs.

She widened her eyes, excited to see them both. She stood waiting to speak since Macky's hands juggled pliers and clamps, all the while he held the horse's long, wiggly, tongue out of the way. Macky wore a hat with a bright light on it that shone right into the stallion's mouth and down his throat. Jackson managed a faint smile, but his eyes looked sad. He held a silver medical bucket full of sanitized tools for his pop.

"Morning, Carson," the horse dentist said while glancing up from his last patient—a black and white pinto with a pot belly. "I can see you've got your good horse manners about ya. Most folks don't know these horses can get spooked pretty easily if someone runs up behind them flailing their arms about. That was a right proper way to approach a horse. Especially one you aren't familiar with."

"Thanks, Macky." Relishing the compliment from the dentist, she squatted down to look at this funny horse at eye level. "And I don't know this one. But Amy Jo's therapy horses won't buck if anyone runs up behind them. They're des-sensit-t-t..."

Macky smoothly joined right in and said the word with her, "desensitized." He looked away from his patient, winked at Carson, then kept working.

"Well, you sure know your horses, young lady. Well done. And I'm glad to hear ya callin' me Macky. All my friends do."

Joy surged through Carson. The horse dentist called her his friend!

Carson turned to Jackson. "You want to meet Goodness?"

"I already have. She was the first one to get her teeth floated."

"Did you see her tricks?"

"No, I didn't see any tricks."

"Macky," Carson said as if asking his permission for something.

"Whatcha need, Miss Kit Carson?" he asked while sanitizing the tools he used in the previous horse's mouth.

Carson smiled. "Can Jackson come see Goodness's tricks?"

"Sure, he can. You two go on." Macky gave his son's shoulder a loving squeeze.

As the two walked around horse trailers and assorted colors of miniature horses, Carson couldn't wait another second to ask about the bad news.

She took a deep breath as they arrived at Goodness' stall, and started in, "What's the bad..." but out of nowhere, Jackson smiled and said, "So show me this little horse's tricks. What can she do? Do I need to take pics of any of the magic that is about to happen here?" He pulled out a brand-new phone.

"Lucky!" Carson yelled the word at him like an accusation. The glimmer in Jackson's eyes was back.

Carson could hardly believe the two of them were going to be taking pictures of these horses on their own with Jackson's brand-new phone. "Let me get her set." She led Goodness into the proper position. "Are you ready to take the pictures?"

"Ready!"

"Goodness, up!" Carson commanded while raising both her arms straight in the air. Goodness did not disappoint.

"Whoa, I can't believe it. She's standing straight up on her hind legs and holding the pose! How long can she stand like that? ...Oh, that long. Can you make her do it again? I didn't get the pic."

"Okay, sure. Tell me when you're ready."

"Ready!" Jackson held the camera out in front of him with his finger ready to touch the camera button.

"Goodness, up!"

"Got it! Wow. What else can she do?"

"Hang on. I'll show you."

"This is radically cool stuff. Maybe I should video this one."

"Let me look at these first," Carson leaned over the phone while Jackson scrolled through a few of the pics. "It can be hard to get good shots of a moving target like Goodness."

"Grrrr," Carson gave a long huff, smiled, then pushed Jackson pretty hard.

"What was that for? And did you just growl at me?"

"Jacks, your photos are amazing. They're perfect. I want a phone like yours so bad!"

Jackson smirked. "Hey, give the photographer some credit. I've got skills. It's not all this spectacular, phenomenal phone." With each word Jackson presented his phone a little closer to Carson like a prized trophy.

Carson never had so much fun being jealous before.

Jackson swiped to another photo. "Oh and hey, look at this beauty!" Carson looked and it was a goofy close up of her telling Goodness to go up.

"Oh, you better delete that one right now!" Carson grabbed the phone and Jackson grabbed it right back. "Jacks, come on, delete it! I look like a llama with sand in its eyes."

Jackson studied the photo. Carson was awkwardly frozen in the middle of the trick. " I would have never seen llama girl in this photo." Jackson said, "but now I can't unsee her."

They both laughed so hard that they started laughing at the way each other was laughing. Then they realized that what they were laughing at wasn't really all that funny, and for some reason, that made them laugh even harder.

By now, it appeared Goodness was tired of all this laughing nonsense. At the end of her series of tricks the humans were supposed to give her a treat after she bowed. Goodness spontaneously curled her left hoof underneath herself and extended her right hoof forward, producing a dramatic pose.

"Oh, my goodness, well, I guess we're done here," Carson said, catching her breath from laughing. "Looks like the final bow of the performance!"

Jackson moved quickly and managed to get it on his phone.

"I bet that comes out blurry," Carson teased. "You were laughing like a crazy person."

"Me? Crazy? What about you? Growling-llama girl!"

The two of them growled and laughed all the way to the office in the barn.

"Hey Carson, did you notice that you didn't stutter at all, not even one time, when you were with Goodness?"

"Yeah, I know, I never stutter around her."

So, Jackson does notice that I have a stutter after all, Carson thought.

As she held the horse's lead rope in one hand and opened the office door with the other, she thought,

Here we go! Jackson's going to see his dream about the next trading card become a reality.

"Uh, llama girl, are you supposed to bring Goodness inside? You might want to tie her up over here first." Carson smiled as big as she ever had, held the door open with her boot and gave a "ta da" gesture with her free arm. The corner of the office was set up for the photo shoot. They both stared at the combat boots and army gear waiting for Goodness to wear.

A somber shadow cast across Jackson's face. "You know, my mom's in the army."

Carson's heart didn't know where to go with her feelings. She thought Jackson would be over the moon about this. She could feel the thickness of his sadness in the room.

"She used to stutter too."

Carson couldn't believe it. His mom used to stutter?

Jackson sat down in the office chair. It was one of those that could spin around. He turned in it and stopped when he was facing the wall.

Carson felt her eyes getting moist with tears, like something heartbreaking had already been spoken.

"My mom's being deployed in three weeks."

Carson froze. *This is it. The bad news.* Carson knew being deployed was serious. But she wasn't exactly sure what it meant, not totally.

Carson walked around the chair, so she could see Jackson's face. It was wet with tears.

"I don't want to talk about it. But I'm glad I told someone."

"Jackson, I don't know what to say."

"It's okay. I don't either."

"Do you still want to do the photo shoot?" Carson asked.

"Yeah. More than ever."

"Good. Let's get this done! Jacks, this is for your mom."

12

Serious as Sugar

"Carrr-sonnn!" her mom hollered from the van in a singsong voice.

Carson and Jackson came darting out from the therapy barn. All the little horses were gone now, so it was no problem for them to dash as fast as they could across the pasture to the driveway. Every now and then one of them jumped for no apparent reason at all as they were running. But, upon closer look it became obvious; they were leaping over tiny little piles of horse poop. Everything about miniature horses was miniature. Even their poop.

Arriving out of breath they found Carson's mom in the middle of inviting Jackson and his pop over for lunch on Easter Sunday.

Oh, please say yes, please say yes, please say yes, Carson kept thinking, as if the more she thought the words, the more likely they were to come true.

"...oh, it's no trouble at all, we're just popping a big ham in the oven," Carson's mom explained. "It won't be anything too fancy. Our family is pretty casual."

Macky held his straw cowboy hat in one hand while wiping his hair back with the other and said, "Well, that's very kind of you and sounds mighty fine. Jackson and I have to head down south tomorrow to a couple of horse farms, then we'll be heading right back through this direction."

"Here's our address. Do you need directions?"

"No ma'am. I'll pull it up on my GPS. I talk to that thing so much I feel like it's a family member."

"I bet you do, going to so many different places around the country every day," Carson's mom responded.

"Mom," Carson said rather quickly trying to catch the conversation before it ended. "Can Jackson and Macky come with us to Easter service?"

Carson's mom looked over at Jackson's dad and then over to Jackson, making sure to include them both in the conversation. "You're more than welcome to come with us. Easter Sunday is always a pretty fun day at church."

"Pop, can we go?"

Oh, please say yes, please say yes, please say yes, Carson continued chanting in her head.

"We're usually on the road Easter Sunday. Aren't we, Jacks? It would be nice to go to a church service for a change." Jackson quickly nodded. Macky placed his hand on the hood of his shiny, black truck. "Now you know we're traveling in this pick-up. We don't carry suits or shiny shoes in there. What'cha see is what'cha get, even on Easter Sunday."

"No problem, Mr. Macky," said Mom. "You two will fit right in."

"We'll be there. And just call me Macky, ma'am. You and your daughter are a lot alike, you know." He grinned and winked Carson's direction.

Carson and her mom turned and walked toward their van when Carson asked, "Mom, what ex-x-actly does it mean to be d-deployed?"

"Deployed?" Mom repeated back to Carson to make sure she had heard her correctly. Carson nodded.

"Oh honey." Mom's eyes began to look sad, "Is Jackson's mom going to be deployed?"

Astounded, Carson thought, *Mom has read between the lines again! Technically, I guess she's listening between the lines. I don't think I have ever heard of that saying before.*

Deciding the metaphor still applied, Carson could tell her mom thought this was bad news too. Yep, real bad news. Her mom stopped talking about anything else and hunched down to Carson's level, looked her in the eyes, and brushed Carson's hair to one side.

"Sweetie...," Mom began.

When adults started using the sweet names, Carson knew things must be serious. Honey, sweetie, and sugar were typical. Carson's grandparents took it to another level with names like sugar dumpling and sugar pie.

"Are you listening, honey?" As Mom continued with her assortment of sweetener names for Carson.

Carson nodded, and wondered which ingredient off the cooking shelf she would be called next.

"Well, sugar, being deployed means his mom will be sent somewhere away from home to serve a tour of duty. In the army that can be a long time."

Carson gave her mom a hard, concerned look while her mouth fell open in shock.

"Do you know where she is going?" Mom asked.

"N-n-no."

"It could be a lot of places these days. Maybe Jackson will tell us more when they come over for dinner on Sunday."

As soon as they buckled up in the van Carson's mom's phone made a chirping sound. They looked at each other for a moment then Carson reached over to pick up the phone.

"Can I look, Mom?" Carson thought it was polite to ask before looking at someone's cell phone. It could be like pushing yourself into people's conversations without saying, "Excuse me."

"Sure, who's it from?"

"It's Jackson. I g-gave him your cell number. It's the p-pics we took with his phone today."

"Jackson has his own phone?" Mom asked.

Carson smirked and nodded in a way that seemed to say, Yep, one more person my age has a phone, while I don't.

Carson's mom leaned over the van's console. "I want to see these, too."

"Mom, Jackson says, 'Wait for it! The last one is the chosen one.'"

"Alrighty, let's see."

The first photo was llama girl. Carson's mom held back a chuckle. "Well, Carson. That's something."

Carson smiled from ear to ear, then furrowed her brow trying to act angry. "Grrr. I told him to delete that one." The rest were all of Goodness in different poses with the army props. Carson and her mom took turns judging each photo as it passed by.

"Too silly."

"Overdone."

"Off center."

"Not bad."

But, when they got to the last one, destined to be the chosen one, they took a long pause. Goodness donned a camo blanket. The American flag hung behind her. Her hooves stood up on a crate right next to some army-issued boots. An official army cap rested on her head. Carson had used her bribing technique with an apple slice to get Goodness still enough for that shot. The results were fantastic. Goodness looked proud and regal.

"That's really moving, Carson."

"Mom, what do you m-mean, moving?"

"It means, the picture is saying so much to me that it's powerful. It actually moves my feelings and thoughts from where they were to another place."

Carson was still trying to understand when her mom explained. "We were scrolling through the photos. We were laughing and feeling generally happy. But then, that particular picture made me suddenly feel proud, sad, angry and happy all at the same time. But mostly proud."

Carson thought, *Wow. I didn't realize one photo could do so much.*

13

Stolen Whinnies

For the first time in weeks, Winter walked from her barn stall into the paddock without feeling worn out. Her skin felt stiff and thick where the stitches had been.

Her instincts were constant task masters. *Don't stay in your stall. It's dark and confined. Get into the open air and breathe.* Once in the pasture, her shoulders softened and her head dropped to graze. The task masters warned, *Stay alert! Be ready to bolt! Ready to bolt!* She quickly lifted her head and pricked her ear to one side.

I'm different now, Winter realized. She looked down the gravel pathway to Doc Browning's house. He used to come out every day at about this time, making sure the herd had plenty of clean water.

I hope Doc stays at the house again today. He used to be my favorite human, but he did a lot of things to my skin and muscles after the mountain lion attack that scared me. Although his body language told me he was being kind and caring, there was pain. I hope he never comes out to the barn again.

Winter was mostly white, but one of her ears was golden brown. That ear stood straight up and turned like a satellite disc. It picked up the sound of two people approaching the barn. One of the voices was a male human. Winter was on edge. *Be ready to bolt, ready to bolt,* her instincts repeated.

"Well, thanks for coming out, Macky," said Mrs. Browning. "All the yearlings are in the east paddock except this one."

Wide-eyed, Winter watched them approach. She heard a deep "woof" as a huge, fluffy-white, slobbery dog circled the humans. Angel, the great Pyrenees, was back on patrol.

The tiny horse relied on Angel's cues. *What is Angel telling me? Head is up, tongue is out and plenty of slobber is hanging from that chin.* Suddenly, Angel turned toward Winter, and they touched muzzle to muzzle. *There it is. Angel has given me the official "friendly visitor" signal.*

Macky's eye caught the two animals squared off nose to nose. "Would ya look at that?" he whispered under his breath. Quickly, he held his cell phone up and snapped a picture. Angel took off to check on the rest of the mini horses. "I work on little horses' teeth every day, and still have a hard time explaining to people how small some of them are. Your guard dog had to bend his neck to look down at that yearling!"

He held up the picture on his phone for Mrs. Browning to see. "Yep" she nodded. "People will get a kick out of seeing a horse smaller than a dog."

This human seems nice, Winter thought, *but so did Doc Browning.* This new human came with a bag of tools to use on the horses, so did Doc Browning. The instincts darted back into her thoughts, *Ready to bolt, ready to bolt.* Winter felt her eyes begin to widen again as she raised her head as high as she could.

"Good golly, Mrs. Browning," Macky said as he hid the tools behind his body. He rested his hands on his knees while crouching down to examine the recovering yearling. "Hey little girl, easy, easy now." Keeping his gaze on the horse he asked, "What tore into this little gal?"

"Oh Macky, it's the saddest thing. The boys at the game commission tracked down and killed a hundred-pound mountain lion. They say it's the one who got her."

"I can't believe it didn't drag her off. It wouldn't have been hard for a lion that size."

Angel sauntered in, back from his herd inspection. "There's our hero," Mrs. Browning said, gesturing toward the large dog. "Our Angel. He kept fighting that cougar until William could get out there."

Macky gave the great Pyrenees some good scratching. Winter relaxed. She was happy to have the dentist's attention diverted.

"What a good dog. Yeah, that's a good boy," he said while Angel rewarded the kind words with thick bands of slobber.

Macky ran his fingers across the scarred areas where Angel had been stitched together by the vet. "Looks like you took a beating, too. Now, let's get a halter on you, little gal, so I can check out your teeth."

Winter began pawing her hoof on the ground while Macky put the halter over her muzzle and buckled it behind her head. "I know you've been through a lot. I don't mind taking it slow."

Winter reared up and tried to whinny as loud as she could. Loud grunts and squeals, sounding much like a pig, came out instead.

Macky looked around. "Yes, Macky," Mrs. Browning confirmed. "Those sounds came from Winter."

###

Macky took off his cowboy hat and gently touched the front of Winter's neck slightly below her jawbone. "Oh man. Don't tell me that devil cat got her vocal cords." A thick mangled-looking scar was forming where the injury had been.

Macky knew this was a great loss. Humans give a lot of admiration and affection to horses because of their majestic and noble sounds. To some degree, this would be a factor in every relationship the horse had from here on out, whether it be with man or beast.

Macky whispered to Winter and himself, "Stolen whinnies." Next, he took account of the other scars by running his calloused fingers over the other stitch marks on Winter's crest and chest. There were a lot to look at.

"Mrs. Browning, I never do this with the little ones, but we're gonna have to sedate or twitch her. The panic and fear in her are too fresh. I recommend twitching over giving her drugs, because all I need is a solid minute to look over the gumline and teeth. If her bite and teeth look even close to good, we'll call it a day for this one. Alright? We can fine tune her bite next time."

Mrs. Browning had already nodded and gone around the corner to get the twitch. "We've had this hanging in the barn forever. I never understood how these things work, and frankly, I have to say I don't like the idea of them." Mrs. Browning surrendered the twitch to the dentist.

"I know, me too," he replied as he clamped the metal device down on the mini's velvety, fat muzzle area below her nostrils. "But, ya sure are grateful for it if you have a panicky horse. She's gonna hurt you and herself while having a hissy fit without it. And right now, she spooks toward anyone who wants to help her."

Mrs. Browning sat down on a wooden stool to watch. "Looky there," she said. "Amazing how she'll let you work on her now. Does it hurt her? 'Cause I gotta say, it kind of looks like it might."

"Nope, she's fine." Macky said while taking a fast yet thorough look over the yearling's teeth and tongue. "And now we're all done." The dentist placed his tools out of the horse's sight. "Her teeth look good. Here's your twitch."

"Mrs. Browning, you know how we always say these mini horses don't know they're little?"

Mrs. Browning chuckled. "Yep, in their little minds, they're Clydesdales and derby champions, the whole lot of 'em."

"This one's been told she's small. And she believes it. It's a real heartbreak to see. But she still has all her beauty and nobility inside. It's written on her DNA. In horse circles we call it God's thumbprint."

Mrs. Browning smiled. "Thanks for coming out, Macky."

"You're welcome, ma'am."

"Macky, you said that yearling's phobia is toward anyone who wants to help her."

"Yes ma'am."

"I've been up here several times and cleaned out her hooves with a pick. My granddaughter cleaned the sutures many times since William lost the strength to leave the house. Winter never gave us a second look. But she did become fearful of William, and you saw how she overreacted to you. Is there any rhyme or reason to her panicky behavior?"

"Yes, ma'am."

Mrs. Browning raised her eyebrows and waited for the answer.

"It's men," Macky said, looking her straight in the eye. "Maybe boys too, I'm not sure. Animals can smell the difference between male and female as easily as you and I can see the difference between cats and dogs.

"Horses respond to the release of pressure. Even if that pressure comes from someone saving their life. In other words, William put a lot of pressure on this little girl by saving her life. He gave her shots and stitches. And now she's mighty confused. It's hard for a horse to understand that the pain was required for the healing."

Mrs. Browning quietly spoke up. "William gave her the best of what he had left, Macky. She got his last breath." Tears welled up in Mrs. Browning's eyes. Macky nodded. They both stared at Winter.

Macky put his hand on Mrs. Browning's shoulder. "William knew there was a grand purpose in saving this little horse. I'm sorry he's not here anymore to see what becomes of this little mare."

Macky drove out to the east pasture to check the rest of the herd. He couldn't help thinking about Winter and how she was now different from the other horses. Would she be more isolated? Horses can be mean to members of the herd that are under stress.

Unexpectedly, his thoughts turned to his son. Jackson had returned to Ft. Bliss in El Paso a few days ago. *Golly, Jacks is about to lose daily contact with his mother for over a year. How's that for stress?*

Doubt he'll be able to stay in El Paso. I only drive out that direction once a year or less. Maybe he'll stay with his Aunt Karen in Chicago. For sure it'll be a new school somewhere. I've seen many kids revert to herd mentality. Bullies pick on the ones under stress. Or the ones under stress become the bullies.

Macky found himself rooting for the little horse deep in his spirit. As if her fate was tied to Jackson's. If a tiny white-haired, blue-eyed horse could overcome a phobia she didn't understand, surely there was hope for Jackson.

14

Full Price

T*welve. I guess I better get used to my new name,* Winter thought as she gave the angry, gray-colored mare plenty of space. Out of the eleven other horses, only the skinny gray one, Number Eleven, spent the days picking on her at this new place with these mismatched strange horses. The others acted like she was invisible most of the time.

Winter's right eye had healed from the cougar scratch a long time ago. But seeing out of it had been cloudy ever since. With Winter's good eye she saw the horses get excited and run toward the green metal gate of the small paddock. A large round hay bale was being rolled through the mud by a stocky lady in rubber boots.

It's hay day! Winter caught the excitement and felt frisky for the first time since the attack.

As she joined the herd to eat, two muddy hooves from Number One, the spotted pony in charge, quickly pounded their way into Winter's shoulder. A few of the other horses glared toward her, ears pinned all the way back. The message was clear: You are new, you are small, you are weak. Twelve, you wait.

The horses were focused on gorging themselves, so Winter had the freedom to search the small paddock for grass without being picked on. She gingerly placed weight on her front right shoulder. It was healed from the cougar attack, but the reprimand from Number One still ached.

Even after it rained for days at Doc and Mrs. Browning's, I never had to pull my hooves out of the mud like this. Winter's thoughts flashed back to her last day at the Browning's horse farm. Was it only months ago? It felt like an eternity.

It had rained at the Brownings' that morning. The lush grass was slightly spongy but easy enough to walk through. Mrs. Browning had tears streaming from her eyes as she thanked the stocky hay lady for lightening her load.

The hay lady had led Winter toward a small trailer as she turned to Mrs. Browning and explained, "I was sitting at home and thought how you must have more than you can handle since Doc passed away. All those animals and land must be a burden to you. I don't know as much about horses as you, but I know how to buy and sell animals on the internet pretty well. This little horse is sure to have ongoing health problems with all that scar tissue and bare skin. It's best you sell her."

Mrs. Browning had placed her shaky, wrinkly, beautiful hands under Winter's chin. "You are a very special little mare. You carry God's fingerprint." She cradled her tiny soft muzzle between her finger and thumb and gave it a few strokes. Mrs. Browning still wore her wedding ring. The diamond cast little reflective dots across Winter's long face.

Then the rusty, blue trailer door closed. The dark noisy ride had led Winter to the small muddy paddock where she had been swiftly told her rank. Twelve.

Two humans approached, causing Winter's instincts to jar her away from the memories of her old home. The familiar chant, *Be ready to bolt. Ready to bolt,* subsided when she realized they were the hay lady and another female.

###

"Your ad says champion bloodlines and excellent conformation in a tiny, crystal-blue-eyed mare, all for $400."

"That's right," the hay lady responded while picking up a lead rope and halter on the way to the paddock. "I'm sorry, what did you say your name was? I've had several texts and calls on this mini horse."

"I'm Amber. The one who texted you from the Austin area. I brought cash and can take her today."

"Great! She's pretty muddy, but I promise under all that dirt she's white as snow."

Amber's heart sank as she saw the seller walk over to the mini horse in the corner, knowing the other horses had alienated her for some reason. Amber was concerned the little horse's knees might buckle from trying to pull her legs up out of the deep muck. Even the hay lady had to work to keep her boots from pulling off into the sticky mess.

As they got closer, Amber's suspicions about the health of the horse went off like sirens before a tornado. *Calm down, Amber,* she thought to herself. *There's a lot of mud on this horse. You won't know what you've got until you really look her over.*

The misty rain clung to Amber's long hair as the temperatures dropped. A late March cold front was coming in. Amber bent down on her knees to look over the shivering horse. As she ran her hand across Winter's bony hips, she noticed scar tissue on her neck and on her crest in a spot where the mane was bare.

Not only has this horse been misrepresented in the advertisement, but she's in desperate condition. Amber felt her heart suddenly consumed with anger. *How can anyone allow this creature to be this way? She needs medical attention that will certainly cost a lot more than the $400 asking price.*

The hay lady could see Amber's disposition change. She quickly pulled out the horse's paperwork. "Look, her double registrations speak for themselves. Her DNA is remarkable, and I'm sure she will produce noteworthy foals when given the chance. She's not mine; I'm helping out her owner who's in over her head right now."

Amber's choking anger would not let her speak. *This horse is a rescue, not a bargain! And money is so tight right now since I lost my job.* Even so, she pulled four $100 dollar bills from her pocket and exchanged them for the miniature horse's paperwork. She grabbed the horse's lead and began quietly walking to her pickup truck.

"Oh great, we have a deal then!" the stocky lady said to Amber's backside. Amber kept walking away.

She couldn't bear to look at the seller who had taken $400 for a horse that was going straight to a vet.

"Horse people are so quirky," the hay lady said under her breath. "Have a nice day!" she hollered at Amber.

Amber loaded the little mare into a mini-sized trailer. The horse slid around inside the trailer, leaving muddy skid marks behind each step. "Alright little one, looks like I'll be driving slow. Try to stay on top of those pine shavings and you'll be fine." Amber cracked a smile as she saw the shaking mini horse gobble down some crunchy clean hay.

Amber climbed up into the tall pick-up truck and pulled the old door shut. She started the engine. Water dripped onto the paperwork in her hands from the stringy wet hair in her face. She read the registrations. "Miniature Horse Name: Winter. Breed: Falabella. Height at the withers: 27 inches, Weight: 100 lbs." The truck rattled as she pulled out onto the main road toward Austin. "My husband's gonna kill me."

15

Easter

"I haven't had an Easter supper like that in ages," Macky said with both hands on his belly. Jackson was in a stare down with the last bit of mac and cheese on his plate.

Carson seemed to notice Jackson's distress and spoke up. "Jacks you don't have to finish everything on your plate. Right Mom?"

"Of course not," she replied while lifting Frannie out of the highchair.

As soon as the toddler's chubby hands were released from her mom's wash cloth, they grasped toward her four-year-old brother. "Bubba, choca-wat. Bubba, choca-wat!"

Mom nodded at Bubba. "You may give her one chocolate candy."

In less than a flash Frannie's tiny feet bounced over to her brother. Her brown eyes blinked wide open as she peered into the basket. But she didn't choose chocolate. With the skill of a domestic cat, she swiped a fuzzy, yellow, wind-up chick toy. She thrust it right up to his nose, causing his eyes to cross as he focused on it. In a somewhat slow, sinister voice, she teased, "Bubba Scooper!" Everyone laughed except Macky and Bubba. They merely smirked.

"I reckon I don't have any idea what that's about," Macky said, "but I've been the butt of many a joke, and I have to say, Bubba, you sure can take it with the best of 'em."

With a proud smile Bubba crossed his arms over his chest and proclaimed, "Yep, I take it all day, every day." Everyone laughed again, even Macky.

Carson's mom offered a brief explanation. "We brought home a lone chick from the farm supply store only to realize that it would probably be killed if we introduced it to an existing brood. Oddly enough, we named him Bubba Scooper—which is another long story."

"Oh yes," Macky nodded. "The pecking order. Did you know horses have something similar? It's called herd order."

Macky watched Carson's mouth drop open as she stared at him in shock. "Carson, remember when we were at the therapy barn working on all those horses?

"Y-Yes."

"Why didn't we throw them all in one big pen together while they waited for me to look at their teeth?"

"Because some of them would p-probably not get along with the others."

"That's exactly right. Even well-behaved, highly-trained therapy horses might bite or kick in that situation. That's how they figure out their rank in the group, their place in the herd."

Carson swallowed hard, "They wouldn't k-kill the weakest ones, would they?"

"That's unlikely. But in a true herd, they pick one to push to the outside. By picking on the weakest, the others are assured that they're superior." Macky's audience was locked on to his every word. This was plain knowledge to him. But few people get to see a large herd of horses living life as they would in the wild.

Mom got up and made her stealthy Sunday-afternoon move. "Joe, will you get out the pies for everyone? I'm going to put these two down for naps." She grabbed a couple of books. "Hey you two, let's go read your favorite stories." They walked down the hallway to the bedrooms.

Macky's chair leg stubbled across the wood floor as he stood up. "Let me help you out there, Joe."

Joe smiled. "Who doesn't want to help with pie, right?" He motioned toward a doorway leading to a small washroom. "I think she has them cooling in there on the washing machine."

Macky saw two pie plates lightly covered with foil. "Yep. Here they are next to the...microscope and... petri dishes? Joe, are there some secret ingredients in these pies I need to know about?" Macky leaned around the laundry room door so Joe could see his sarcastic grin.

Joe chuckled. "Carson's science experiments. Let's hope they didn't end up in the pies."

Macky looked over the pecan and apple pies then held them up. "If they did, science never looked so delicious."

Meeting over the kitchen counter, Joe handed Macky the pie knife. "If you wouldn't mind doing the honors of cutting those pies, I'll make us some coffee—if I can find it." He began digging around in the pantry.

"Oh, wait a sec, Joe. Here ya go." Macky turned on the bright flashlight from his phone and held it in the dark pantry for Joe.

"Oh, here it is. Thanks, Macky. I never think to use the phone flashlight thing. Carson keeps reminding me about it, and she doesn't even have a phone. Somehow, she sure knows how to use every function on mine."

"I know whatcha mean, Joe. When I was their age, our family had one phone attached to the wall in the hallway."

"Macky, let me guess. It had a real long, curly cord connected to the wall, so everyone could take turns using it in their own rooms."

"That's exactly right. We put our finger on a number and literally dialed each number one at a time."

"Yep, rotary dial! If I was lucky enough to have a girl give me her number, by the time I dialed all the numbers, she'd already moved on to my best friend." Both men laughed.

"I think a new phone used to cost about $15. You know, Carson wants a phone. Does Jackson have one?"

"Yep, he sure does. Just got a new one. I'm afraid it was a tad more than $15. But his mom and I thought it was a smart thing to do considering all the stuff he'll be using it for. Did you see the new Support our Troops trading card they put together?"

"Yeah." Carson's dad put his hands in his jeans, waiting on the coffee to finish brewing. "I gotta say, that was really well done."

"The kids did all of it with Jackson's phone."

"Really?"

"Yep, and with Carson loving science like she does, I gotta tell ya, there are some amazing apps out there for identifying all kinds of stuff. Everything from plant life to microbes. I use them myself.

"Jackson flies back and forth from his mom's in El Paso to the different cities where I work. So, I like having the ability to track him in case he gets lost at an airport or somewhere."

Carson's dad took his phone out of his back pocket and looked it over. "I'm supposed to be getting a new phone before long. I never thought I'd hear myself say this, but maybe I should think about letting Carson have this one."

Macky took a big whiff of the cinnamon and sugar mixture baked on top of the pies. "Oh, boy. These sure smell good. I may have to eat more than usual, in the name of science of course!" He glanced back into the utility room at Carson's science equipment. "School sure has changed for kids these days. Now they're coming home from school with microscopes and growing things in petri dishes."

Joe shook his head, "Other than technology, I think schools are mostly the same. But Carson takes all her classes from home these days. Her mom is taking a break from her biology professor career at the university. The two of them practically devour anything pertaining to science, especially animal science. There's always some experiment going on around here. It may involve growing fungus in a petri dish, or saving a small creature found by the creek bed. I can't keep up with those two."

Macky thought back to when he was in eighth grade. "Man, I would have loved that as a kid. I spent most of my days in the classroom staring out the window or getting in trouble. It probably had to do with sitting in that dadgum desk all day."

Joe leaned on the counter while steam escaped the brewing coffee maker. "I guess that makes sense. Look what you do for a living now—traveling around the countryside from barn to barn. It seems like the farthest thing from a desk job."

Macky chuckled. "Yep, working in an office all day would kill me. Although some of the looks I get from these little horses make me think they'd like that honor."

Joe returned a smile. "Carson sure loves those ornery horses. You may have noticed she has a speech impediment. But, maybe not. For some reason, she rarely stutters around the horses."

Macky cut the pies. "My ex-wife, Jackson's mom, used to stutter just like Carson. The army almost didn't let her in because of it. Isn't that something? They're sure glad they let her in now. She handles tactical international money. I don't know what all she does. It's kind of hush, hush. But Jackson calls her the army's money ninja."

"She might be similar to Carson. Carson's mind zips beyond what her speech can keep up with. Every now and then she'll throw out words most kids don't learn until high school."

Macky spoke up. "Oh, I've heard a few doozies!"

Carson's dad stood up tall, looking shocked.

"Don't worry, none of 'em were inappropriate. Heh, heh. Just big 'ol meaningful words."

Joe relaxed. "We didn't want to slow the kid down. By homeschooling through the university, her mind can keep zipping forward."

"A university? She's taking college classes?"

"No, no, they're middle school classes, except science. She's a grade ahead in science," Joe explained. "The university has its own middle and high school programs online."

Carson's mom walked into the kitchen just as Macky's phone went off. Buzz, buzz, buzz.... Handing the cut pies to Carson's mom, he kindly nodded his head. "Excuse me, I'm just going to look at this real quick." Macky typed a response then put the phone back in his pocket.

"Do you think Carson would like to assist Jackson and me on a quick dental appointment?"

"Are you kidding? She'd love it," Joe said, placing coffee mugs for everyone on the countertop.

"I don't normally work on holidays. This lady just texted me saying she heard I was in town. She rescued a little horse and thinks it was attacked by a pack of dogs. Now don't be alarmed, the attack happened a couple hundred miles from here. And the little horse is doing fine now."

Carson's dad was re-thinking his answer. "I don't think Carson has enough time to travel a couple hundred miles from here."

"Oh, no, the lady lives ten minutes away. The horse was attacked before she bought it. She wants me to look over the mouth real well, to make sure there aren't any dental issues. I think the whole visit won't take more than an hour. Might as well do it while I'm in town."

Carson chased Jackson into the kitchen, running into the counter and knocking over some trash from the overstuffed bin. She darted left then right and tagged Jackson on the back. "Not it!"

Jackson looked at the trash can, drawing in Carson's attention, and replied, "Tsk. Tsk."

Carson looked at her parents and picked up the spilt trash. Jackson turned on a dime and gave her a push. "Not it!"

As he sprinted away Carson got him right back. "Not it!"

Macky looked serious. "Aren't you two turkeys a little old for that game?"

Carson's dad chimed in, "Macky, I guess you better take these two outside and put them to work. They seem to need someplace to use all that energy. Maybe they'd like to help out a little horse down the road who needs a dental exam."

Carson turned to face Macky, stood tall and confident, and dramatically placed her hands on her hips. "Heck, yeah. I'll help."

Before Carson's hair could even sway with her response, Jackson had made his move. He tapped his finger on top of her head from behind and with a wink to everyone in the room proclaimed, "Not it! I'll be in Pop's truck!" And out he flew.

16

Kit Carson

Carson hoisted herself into the large backseat of Macky's pick-up truck. *Wow! It looks like a road trip party exploded back here.* She gazed at packages of cheese crackers and trail mix on the floor board, fleece blankets and hand-held video games.

After Macky's phone synced up with the truck's GPS, Jackson piped up from the front passenger seat, "This horse farm's only eight miles away.

Macky peered in the rear-view mirror making eye contact with Carson. "You know, I saw your fungus experiment in the utility room."

Without missing a beat Jackson quipped, "Hey Pop, Mom said the exact same thing to me the other day, but I'm pretty sure she was talking about my socks."

A sudden burst of laughter hit Macky so fast that his lips popped open and some spit hit the windshield.

Carson giggled.

Staring at the spit as it clung to the windshield, Jackson made his eyes extra wide on purpose and smirked, "Maybe we can get some fungus out of that. Eh, Pop?"

Then he turned to Carson and quietly mouthed, "So gross."

Carson held her breath in an effort to stop laughing. *I don't want Macky to think I'm laughing at him. But Jacks is killing me.*

Macky wiped off the windshield with his sleeve and said, "Alright you two, buckle up."

While riding on the main road, Carson peeked up at Jackson, who seemed pleased with himself. In the rear-view mirror, she could see the reflection of Macky's comfortable smile. *This must be how it goes between these two when they travel. I love it,* she thought.

Macky continued, "Anyway young lady, I was just going to say, I think it's great that you enjoy biology and science experiments so much."

"Hearing you s-speak on horses' t-teeth was part of my animal s-science." Carson paused. She wanted to say, Hearing you speak on horses' teeth was part of my animal science *assignment.* Although her speech had improved a lot this year, that particular word still got caught on the way out of her mouth. And when that happened, it didn't sound like a very nice word. *The curse of knowing great words, but only using them in my heart.* The thought came and went in her head many times a day.

Macky casually smiled, "I remember that day. You said you were named after Kit Carson." She sat up tall and nodded. The horse dentist continued, "I was in Colorado a few summers back and went to the Buffalo Bill Museum. Did you know Buffalo Bill named one of his kids after Kit Carson?"

Jackson turned toward Carson. "How cool is that?"

Macky paused to listen to his GPS direct him onto a small country road. He continued, "I found it interesting that when Buffalo Bill was a young man, he met an old guy who was highly intelligent, yet soft spoken. He had been an Indian scout for the government. He knew several Native American languages and used his skills to help people. This person was Carson, Kit Carson."

Carson fidgeted with the leather handle on the side of the truck door while her mind envisioned a man in leather pioneer clothes riding a horse. She too loved horses and was soft spoken. It was a powerful moment, realizing she had more in common with the historical person than just her name.

Jackson asked, "Did Buffalo Bill's son have a lot in common with the real Kit Carson?"

"I don't know about that, but little Kit Carson did travel with his dad in the Buffalo Bill show. And that show made a big difference in how people thought about each other and treated each other around the world. Nowadays we would say his show had a good humanitarian impact."

Carson leaned to the side so she could see the horse dentist's eyes in the rear-view mirror.

Macky continued, "People everywhere wanted to know what the wild west was like. There was no TV or internet. So, he packed up horses, cattle, bison, and lots of different kinds of people. He even took the wild west show to Europe."

Jackson looked at his dad. "Kind of like a circus?"

"I guess it was in some ways."

Carson was thinking hard. She didn't like circuses. Putting animals into cages and making them travel around bothered her. Animals like to be free to roam.

"Buffalo Bill got a lot of people worked up too. Because he felt it was important to pay everyone in his show the same for their hard work, even women. Native Americans, African Americans, and people from very poor cultures were treated equally. He took a lot of heat for that.

"Listen to this, Jacks; he even had a freak show. And I know the idea of that probably bothers you." Jackson wrinkled his eyebrows, looking upset with the notion.

Carson leaned forward. "What w-was the freak show?"

"People who had genetic defects—physical features that made them appear different—were the stars of that show."

"That doesn't sound humanitarian," Jackson said.

"Son, you gotta understand, back in the 1800s it was a different world. People that had rare genetic traits like hair that grew thick all over their bodies, or extra skin that was super stretchy, or who were Siamese twins, were destined for poverty back then. No one would hire them. Buffalo Bill didn't just give them jobs, he gave them equal pay and an equal say in his show."

Jackson interrupted, "Wait, what are Siamese twins?"

"That means two people were born sharing some of the same body parts. The proper way to address them these days is conjoined twins. When I was a kid, they were called Siamese twins. I think that was because the most famous set was from Siam."

Jackson could hardly speak.

Macky explained, "Buffalo Bill knew these folks to be smart, witty, and just like anyone else. He felt compelled to offer them a way to make a decent living. I'll tell ya, that was quite the scandal back then."

"Why, Pop?"

"They looked different, so it made people uncomfortable. It was hard for them to get jobs. And without jobs, they didn't have money. And without money, they couldn't buy food, have families, or pay for a place to live."

Carson sat quietly. *If I lived in the 1800s, I wonder if I would have been poor because I stutter. I look pretty normal, but I don't sound like everyone else. Maybe I could have worked for Buffalo Bill. I am sure he would have liked me.*

Jackson searched Buffalo Bill on his phone. "Buffalo Bill! Yep, here he is." Jackson dramatically raised one of his eyebrows as if speaking to a crowd off into the distance and proclaimed, "I'm going to have a daughter one day and name her after Buffalo Bill. She shall be..."

As if on cue, Carson began a drum roll with her hands on the leather seat in preparation for the announcement.

"... Buffalo McClellan!"

Carson grinned. "Yeah! You could c-call her Buffy Mack for short." As if reading each other's minds, they spontaneously started making beatbox noises and spitting out lyrics between carefully timed lip pops.

Macky shook his head. "How in the world did we go from discussing history and humanity to rapping? Yo, my name is Buffy Mack and you know bro, I got your back!"

A chime sounded and a notification from Macky's phone popped up on the truck's display. It was from Jackson's mom.

My sister in Chicago said he can stay with her.

"Pop. What does Mom mean?" Jackson asked, no longer acting silly.

"Jacks, don't worry about that. We can talk about it later."

"It's about me. Isn't it?"

"Jacks, you know my job won't let me stay in one place. You're going to probably stay with your aunt while your mom's deployed in Germany."

"Pop, no," Jacks said in uncharacteristic defiance. "I don't want to go to Chicago for one or two years!" Jackson's eyes began to tear up.

"I want to hear how you feel about this son, but we'll have to talk about it later."

Jackson didn't respond. He sunk deep into the

seat, pulled his knees up under his chin and wrapped his arms around them. He watched out the window as unfamiliar roads and houses flew by.

Carson had an overwhelming urge to hug him, hold his hand, and tell him it was ok. But she felt like any of those things would be wrong right now. So, she put those feelings on a shelf in her mind, and began to problem solve.

Why would he have to live with his Aunt in Chicago? Why couldn't he live with his Pop?

Because Macky traveled at least once every week. A kid can't go to school and have friends when traveling on the road like that. Or can he?

17

Winter's Mercy

Carson was thinking. *I need the perfect word for today.* She reflected as she and Jackson followed Macky to greet the owner at the barn. *I've spent the day with Jackson and now here I am in a miniature horse breeder's pasture. Not only that, I'm assisting the famous miniature-horse dentist on a visit!*

Hmmm. I'm sad for Jacks, but at the same time, I'm doing all my favorite things today. Is one word capable of holding all of that?

Several mares grazed around a large bale of hay. Each had a foal that frolicked about. Carson felt a strong connection to the horses and mused at how the scene looked like neighborhood parents sharing the latest news and opinions, while the kids played freeze tag in the yard.

"So, which one is my patient?" Macky asked.

Amber, the owner, pointed away from the horse activity to a far corner in the pasture. "She's up there staying out of the sun."

Carson touched Jackson's arm, "J-Jacks, she's all alone." The horse's ears popped straight up. One was white like the rest of the horse. The other ear, turned toward them, was golden brown. The white horse had what appeared to be a mask covering her eyes and face. Macky carried his stainless-steel medical bucket in one hand. With each step, the liquid disinfectant sloshed in the bottom of the bucket while the heavy tools slid around inside.

The mask was blue and slightly oversized for her tiny head. *Poor little horse. Maybe her face is disfigured from the dog attack.* The disturbing stories about the freak shows from the 1800s were still fresh in Carson's mind. She wondered if the other horses treated this mare like an outsider.

Carson boldly looked up at Amber. "D-does she have to wear the mask? I d-don't care what she looks like under it."

Amber smiled and pulled apart the mask's Velcro strips in order to remove it. "Her name is Winter. This is just a fly mask." As the horse breeder gently took off the covering, Carson could see how bare and pink the horse's skin was. "Her scars can sunburn easily, and that could lead to skin or eye cancer. But Winter doesn't seem to care whether the mask is on or off."

Macky knelt down to carefully look over the mare. She was about 27 inches tall at her shoulders. He ran his hands over the scars on her neck. "I've seen this horse before. Dogs didn't do this."

Amber pulled up a barn stool and sat close to Macky, as if ready to hear a good story. The dentist continued his exam. First, he separated the horse's thick lips to inspect her teeth. Then he grabbed her long, pink tongue and pulled it to one side to inspect molars.

"This tiny mare survived a mountain lion attack."

Carson looked at Jacks to see his reaction. He mouthed the words, "What? No way!"

"Frankly, I'm surprised she's so relaxed. Did you give her anything to calm her down for the tooth float?"

"Nope. Not a thing. She's such a good, little, calm horse."

"Well, she wasn't after the attack."

Amber had a proud look about her. "She was a mess when I bought her. I had to take her straight to the equine hospital. After a week, we introduced her to the herd slowly and gave her plenty of space. We didn't place any expectations on her. I guess you could say we gave her space to reconnect with her equine soul."

The dentist stuck his float tool into Winter's mouth and began to shave the sharp edges off her molars. "You've certainly earned my respect. You've done a mighty good job." He paused and pulled out what looked like a huge part of her tooth.

Carson blurted out, "W-what just happened?"

Macky pulled out another, and gave it to Carson to hold. "These are her wolf teeth. They're like our baby teeth. It means she's pretty young. In fact, she has some in there that aren't ready to come out yet."

Carson studied the tooth cap as if it were a fine gemstone.

"This horse belonged to Doc Browning before he passed away. I know you said you got her out of a bad situation. But Doc and his wife doted on their minis. I'd always said if I'd been born a miniature horse, I'd sure hope to live at Doc Browning's. That place was practically heaven. Doc's last act of kindness was saving this mare. The vet told him to put her down. She was pretty far gone."

Carson stared tenderly at Winter's scars, now knowing they were once gashes from a cougar's claws and fangs. *Oh Winter, what have you been through? You are such an amazing little thing.*

Amber probed, "What happened to Doc Browning?"

"He passed away from lung disease." Macky kept talking as he finished filing the horses' teeth. "But being a doctor, he knew how to save her. And he did."

Amber spoke up. "The lady I bought Winter from wasn't named Browning. She had about a dozen horses in a small muddy pen. Winter had bite marks on her hide. Most likely she'd spent the days being cornered by the others."

The dentist put his tools into the bucket of disinfectant and wiped his hands on a clean towel. "I sure hate to hear that. Sounds to me like all those horses were stressed. You know as well as I do, in a herd under stress, negative energy is going to come out somewhere." Macky peered down at Winter. "I guess they took it out on the weakest link here."

Amber stood up. "Come to think of it. The seller did say she was selling these for a friend of hers who had too much to handle."

Macky set his jaw off to one side. "It's a darn good thing you got this one out of there."

Carson pressed her face up to Winters soft squishy muzzle. *What a journey you've had at such a young age.* Winter leaned in and huffed some air out her nostrils and into Carson's face.

"Look Pop, Carson's getting horse kissed!" Macky and Amber chuckled. Carson's heart lifted with delight.

"Now you've got to return the favor, Carson," Jackson said. "Exhale into her nostrils."

Carson took a deep breath and exhaled into the horse's funny nostrils. They were shaped like commas. Winter closed her eyes and made a quiet smacking sound with her lips and tongue.

Macky turned to Amber. "What made you decide to buy Winter? Sounds like she was quite an expense for you. A week-long stay at the equine hospital ain't cheap. She's gonna need special attention the rest of her life."

"The advertisement said her dam and sire were prized show horses. Her entire lineage was listed. It was impressive, and the price reasonable. When I got there, I was shocked by what I saw. I couldn't leave her. Her eyes were empty, like she was about to give up."

"If you ever decide to breed her, those gorgeous genetics and DNA are gonna shine through."

Jackson got down on his knees and stroked Winter's muzzle. "God's thumbprint. Right Pop?"

"I've heard of that with animals," Amber said. "What is it?"

"All living creatures have DNA that reflects God's image. It's like his signature on them. And this miniature horse, torn up as she is, is no exception."

Carson's eyes were still fixated on Winter. "The thumbprint of God," she whispered, feeling connected with the little horse's soul. "I see it now, Winter. You're gorgeous."

Winter's owner smiled. "Well, you guys gotta see this, then." She put her thumb and finger in her mouth and whistled in the direction of her house.

Her husband hollered back, "What is it?"

"Hey! Bring over the foal!"

Carson and Jackson gazed across the pasture to see which foal he would bring. But Macky looked in a different direction—under Winter's belly. "Well, I'll be darned."

"What is it, Pop?"

Macky raised his eyebrows. "She's bagged up with milk."

Amber smiled. "We like to say, Winter blew in this year with a little surprise."

The tiniest of foals with the exact same color patterns as Winter and crystal-blue eyes zoomed toward them in a zigzag pattern.

Winter greeted her baby from across the pasture with bizarre grunts and squeaks.

"What was that?" Jackson asked. "It sounded like a pig. Did that squealing come from Winter?"

Macky bent down and put his hands on his knees to examine her throat. "I remember that sound from Doc's." He ran his fingers over the scar on her throat. "Her vocal cords healed up real nice. I reckon that's her unique whinny now."

Amber watched the mom and foal touch muzzles and take in each other's breath. "We think she sounds adorable. Mercy comes running from wherever she is when she hears it. None of the other foals will mistake that for their mom's whinny."

Carson looked at Macky and Jacks and quietly exclaimed, "Oh Mercy! Aren't you miraculous and marvelous?" Even Carson was a little taken back by how easily those long words that she thought so often rolled off her tongue so all could hear.

Carson sensed Jacks and Macky were at peace watching Winter, free to be herself. Mercy darted around them. Carson's mind and heart wouldn't rest. She still had not found the perfect word for how she felt. She needed it, like a musician needs words for his song. *Can one word hold joy, and peace along with a sense of really needing things to work out so hearts don't get broken?* Carson thought. *There must be, there has to be.*

She looked into one of the miniature horse stalls and saw a circle cut out of the door about the size of a paper plate.

"Miss Amber, why is that hole in the stall door?"

"That's so they can see out, and more importantly, see the sunrise."

"I've never heard horses need to see the sunrise."

"Carson, there's never been a night that could defeat a sunrise or a problem that could defeat hope."

Hope! Carson thought. *That's it!*

18

Hope

A chubby, gray-speckled mini horse began to pace the fence line in front of Winter and neigh. Occasionally, the speckled mare would stop, shake her head, and pound the ground with her hoof.

Carson, free from the usual constraints of words getting caught on her tongue, began asking questions.

"Miss Amber, why is the mare acting that way? Is she your boss mare?"

"That's right, Carson. She's the one in charge of the herd. She doesn't like it when Mercy's away from her too long."

Mercy gobbled up milk from Winter. The dam and foal seemed content and unaffected by the boss mare's frustration.

Amber pointed to the frustrated, speckled boss mare. "That's Dancie. She was supposed to have a foal due on Good Friday. Unfortunately, the foal didn't make it." Carson was crushed. Amber said, "Sometimes these things happen with horses. It's sad, but part of life."

Macky looked concerned. "Is the boss mare trying to take over Winter's foal? I've seen horses who lost their babies try to steal away other babies in the herd."

Amber smiled. "I've seen that happen with other horses too. But I've never heard of anything like what's happening here. The two mares share Mercy."

Jackson started videoing the horses with his phone. Carson eagerly asked more questions. "What do you mean, they share her?"

"Dancie is like the beloved auntie who lets you have whatever you want. Because Dancie is the boss mare of the herd, none of the other horses are allowed to correct Mercy or push her aside."

Jackson looked away from his phone for a second. "Because Dancie thinks Mercy is hers, right?"

Before Amber could answer Carson added, "Don't all the horses in the herd have a position? A kind of rank? So, if Dancie is the number one horse, are you saying Mercy is number two?"

"Actually, Dancie has claimed Mercy as her own. That means the foal is like an extension of herself. Dancie's made sure that all the other horses know Mercy is entitled and expected to be treated like the boss mare." Amber chuckled and pointed at Mercy. "This half-pint runs the show around here, literally!"

Everyone snickered.

Under his breath Macky quoted, "...and a little child shall lead them."

Dancie gave out a low neigh and pounded her hoof on the metal gate. Mercy lifted her head as if she were a regal thoroughbred, though she barely came up to Macky's knees.

"Go on, Mercy," Carson encouraged. "Your Auntie Dancie is calling." As if on cue, Mercy ran to the grey-speckled mare. Amber's husband opened the gate for Mercy and she ran off alongside Dancie.

Carson glanced back at Winter, "Will Winter be sad here alone?"

"Look at her face. Does she look sad?"

"No. Oh my goodness... is she smiling?"

"Yeah, that's a thing she does."

Jackson whipped out his phone, stuck it below Winter's face and took a picture. After glancing at it, he quickly displayed it for all to see. "Yep, the camera loves her."

Amber added, "Winter's free to go in with the other horses whenever she likes. They all get along well. She's found her place with them."

Macky looked at his watch. "Alright kids, we gotta go."

Carson exhaled. "Oh, I just love that little Mercy."

Macky put his hand on Carson's shoulder. "Carson, the way you speak so easily around this little horse is nothing short of a miracle. Maybe your folks will let you buy her."

Amber shook her head. "Nope. Sorry guys. She's already been spoken for. She's gonna be a therapy horse."

Carson blurted out, "Jackson! What if she's going to Miss Amy's?"

Amber nodded. "Yes. She is. Amy's the one who bought her."

Carson's mind began to reel. "That means I'll get to help train her. I'll get to watch her grow up! Jacks, we can put her on a trading card like we did with Goodness!"

"Holy cow," Macky said. "Goodness and Mercy in the same therapy barn. Now I've heard everything."

Amber walked with them to the truck. "So, who's Goodness?"

Jackson dug in his jacket pocket and pulled out what looked like a deck of cards, except each card was identical. "Here ya go. We make therapy-horse trading cards for Miss Amy. The horses are kind of like local celebrities around here. Folks like to collect them."

"We just made this one for Memorial Day and Veteran's Day," Carson said, pointing to the picture of the copper-colored horse in Army gear.

Amber said under her breath, "Oh my goodness."

Jackson and Carson shared a knowing glance. People almost always said that when they saw the card, not even knowing the horse was actually named Goodness.

Amber stared at the card for quite a while. She read it out loud. "Support our Troops." She giggled at the tiny sorrel horse looking so dignified in uniform. Then she flipped it over and read, "We remember."

"Very cool, Jackson. My husband is going to love this. He was serving overseas when I bought Winter."

"Here. You can have one for him too." Jackson handed her more. "In fact, here are some for your friends."

"This means more than you know. Thanks, Jackson."

Jackson's smile faded. He stood somber and tall. "My mom's about to be deployed. This card is for her, and your husband, and anyone else in the military."

###

Winter looked at Amber and the three visitors as they walked back to the gate. Something was familiar about the dentist. She wanted to remember what it was. Taking off in a trot, she quickly got behind him and bit at his back pocket with her lips. Her nose quickly picked up the scent of his leather wallet. Unable to resist, she grabbed it with her teeth, then dropped it to the ground.

Macky's hand felt his empty back pocket. "I've never seen such a thing." He pivoted on the heels of his boots and crouched to the ground. Gathering his wallet, he looked the tiny pickpocket in the eyes.

"I have a feeling she remembers you," Amber said.

Winter's thoughts honed in on that wallet. *I've seen and smelled that before.*

Macky's low soothing voice was familiar indeed. "Hey there, little one. So glad you remembered me. Remember ol' Doc? Remember your guard-dog, buddy—Angel? That big dog fought hard for you the night the cougar got ya. And guess what? Angel made it. He's fine."

Winter thought hard. She didn't understand what the dentist was talking about. But right now, she remembered this kind man. And she trusted him.

Jackson chimed in, "Pop, you told me one of the great things about horses is they live in the moment.

You said they don't carry all the sadness of the past around with them."

"That's right, son. I'm real proud of ya for rememberin' that. Living in the moment means they don't worry about the future either."

Macky put his arm around his son. "Jacks, I know you're worried about the future. I don't know if you'll end up taking classes online from a university like Carson does or go to live with your Aunt." Jackson kept stroking Winter's mane. All three kept their gaze on Winter instead of looking at each other.

Macky went on, "This little horse has been through a lot. And look how great she's doing. And she didn't even have family to help her. We have each other to get through this. Surely, we can figure this out."

Jackson and Carson gave Winter a final hug. Jackson ran his fingers down Winter's mane and across the scars on her neck.

Winter had the sense she was making an unbearable moment bearable. And she didn't mind. In fact, she enjoyed the quiet attention.

Amber softly smiled. "I think Mercy will be a great therapy horse—if she's anything like her mama, Winter."

Winter felt the edgy uncomfortable feelings from the humans melting off like icicles in the sunshine. Although she didn't know what all the emotions were exactly, she sensed when they melted, they left puddles behind that felt pure, fresh and honest.

Winter let out a deep sigh and smiled. *Now that we all have Mercy, anything can happen.*

Acknowledgements

First and foremost, I must thank my husband and best friend, Bryan. When I went nuts over miniature horses as an adult, you could have sent me for intensive counseling; instead, you bought me a tiny mare named Goodness.

Secondly, this book would never have been completed without other writers' support. To my very first writing partner, Tiffany White, thank you. And to the Water Oak Writer's Group: Brenda O'Bannion, Cheryl Waugh, Donna Looper, Bruce Hammack, Lori De Jong and Teresa Lynn, I am most grateful. Your wise counsel and harsh edits were life's breath to me. And Teresa, your extra time as professional editor and advisor was invaluable. Thank you to my daughter-in-law, Zoe Threlkeld, for being so well-read in this genre and willing to pick over each character.

Thank you, Brenda and Randy Salley, for sharing your lake house, where much of my writing was clicked out late at night.

I'm indebted to Pat and Vick Kennedy. They graciously offered Goodness and Mercy safekeeping until we had a barn of our own. Many of the magical stories from that old barn will be in the prequel to *Stolen Whinnies.* Thank you to the many volunteers and supporters of the nonprofit Miniwonders, where Goodness and Mercy shined as therapy horses for years.

Jennifer, Terry, and Abby Sims, thank you for taking ownership of the little divas, Goodness and Mercy, so I could have time to write their stories for everyone's enjoyment and inspiration.

Thank you, Julie Ragland, Mercy's compassionate and knowledgeable breeder. And thank you, Jay Pennington, Doctor of Anesthesiology, for your insight into the character, Doc Browning. Brig. General Paul T. Weyrauch, your assistance in understanding the U.S. Army structure, lifestyles and especially the Army's respect of horses brought much confidence to my writing on the subject. Thank you.

Dad—although you're gone, I can still hear your voice whenever I back up a horse trailer in tight spaces saying, "You got this!" Ongoing gratitude goes to my mom and sons for loving me as I care for all the animals and continue to dream more dreams.

Most of all thanks to my savior Jesus Christ, for allowing me to be part of the healing he offers to us all. There was no stumbling into this beautiful story, only providence.

About the Real Horses of Stolen Whinnes

To find out more about the real miniature horses of *Stolen Whinnies* and if they may be coming to a town near you, follow Wendi Threlkeld's author sites.

fromtheranchwithlove.com
Instagram: @fromtheranchwithlove

Stolen Whinnies is also available on audible and ebook formats. Information on websites above.

Made in the USA
Las Vegas, NV
20 April 2021